The King of Siam

The King of Siam

Murray Logan

The Porcupine's Quill

CANADIAN CATALOGUING IN PUBLICATION DATA

Logan, Murray, 1958–
The King of Siam

ISBN 0-88984-195-0

1. Title.

PS8573.O3376K56 1998   C813'.54   C98-930208-3
PR9199.3.L63K56 1998

Published by The Porcupine's Quill,
68 Main Street, Erin, Ontario NOB ITO.
Readied for the press by John Metcalf; copy edited by Doris Cowan.
Typeset in Galliard, printed on Zephyr Antique Laid,
and bound at The Porcupine's Quill Inc.

The cover is after a photograph by Murray Logan.

This is a work of fiction. Any resemblance of characters to persons,
living or dead, is purely coincidental.

Represented in Canada by the Literary Press Group. Trade orders are
available from General Distribution Services.

We acknowledge the support of the Ontario Arts Council,
and the Canada Council for the Arts for our publishing program.
The financial support of the Government of Canada
through the Book Publishing Industry Development Program
is also gratefully acknowledged.

1 2 3 4 • OO 99 98

For my mother and father

I would like to thank Diane Schoemperlen, *The New Quarterly*,
and, especially, John Metcalf.

Thank you also to the Canada Council Explorations Program
for its financial assistance.

And thanks to my friends for their support.

Contents

Everett and Evalyne

THE BUS DRIVER WAITS until I am seated before she pulls away from the curb. They're not supposed to do that but some of them will. So that's a little gift, I suppose. She also calls me 'dear', which is something else. She means well by it.

It's mid-morning and the bus is not at all crowded. Which means no one feels obliged to stand, to give me his seat. I am always grateful when they do, who would not, but I always feel a certain – I don't know. As if something were being given and taken away at the same time.

Today is my birthday. I'm on my way to buy myself a birthday present. If you have no one else to do it, then you do it for yourself. And now I am feeling sorry for myself. I will *not* feel this way. No one likes a little old lady with a cross on her shoulder. Not even me.

I like to watch people, which is a blessing since I have no alternative to the bus. Not that I use it that often. I tend to stay in my own neighbourhood; I know all the little stores, a lot of the shopkeepers know me. A neighbourhood is like a little town, I imagine.

But today I am taking the bus downtown to buy myself a surprise. And on the way I watch the people on the bus. It seems that a different sort of person rides the bus these days. Everyone who can afford one operates a car, I suppose. You see teenagers – they're wearing their hair short again, which is a relief. Although that seems to upset a number of people, the very short hair. I think that it's a nice change from that hippy look you used to see. Perhaps it's the girls wearing it that way. It used to be that you couldn't tell if that young person with all the hair was a boy or a girl, and now it's the other way around. Still, I think that short is better than long. Cleaner, for one thing.

I get off the bus outside Eaton's. As I walk along the sidewalk I know that people, without even really looking, see in me what they choose to see: another blue-haired old lady in crêpe-soled shoes. I know this. But I can't afford to slip and fall – I've seen the results.

And would you rather see hair that is yellowed and stained, like the bottom of someone's ashtray? The blue keeps it neat. Although I must say that I never thought that I'd be one of them.

I know where the shop is but I can't quite bring myself to go directly there. So I sit on a bench for a few minutes, enjoying the spring sunshine. I'm wearing one of those dresses you always see us wearing, as well. But what else could I wear? Slacks? A pair of jeans? Better to be quietly predictable than ridiculous, I think. Even if I didn't think, you cannot escape who you are. You might not like it particularly, but there you go.

The beggars on the street bother me. Not for the reasons you'd think, but because I don't know how much I should give them. When the price of coffee is a dollar, should that be the correct amount? It seems a lot to me, though. I drop a quarter into a man's hat and feel vaguely guilty all the way to the end of the block. And then I stand and fret, thinking that I should go back and give him something more. But the light changes, and I cross the street.

I stand outside the shop, fidgeting with my purse. The door, and the large window that faces the street, are frosted, so I can't see in. I read the sign again: Mother's Tattoos. I smile, mostly at myself. I'm not supposed to know that such places exist. I'm supposed to have spent my entire life knitting and putting up preserves.

I open the door and step inside.

It's like the doctor's. Chairs, a coffee table, neat stacks of magazines. I cannot tell you the disappointment I feel. It's empty, but someone calls from the next room – a doorway is there, blocked off by a bamboo screen – telling me that he'll be right with me. I sit and look around.

The walls are covered with samples of tattoos. Sheets of paper or cardboard, each with a different design on it. I stand up and walk closer. Tigers, skulls, naked women carrying large swords that drip blood. Roses seem to be popular. I sit down again.

Two men come through the door, one of them hardly more than a boy. The boy, the teenager I suppose, leaves by the front door, so I am left alone with the other man. He's huge, tall and broad, though he's gone to fat, as many of that sort will. He has long hair tied back in a ponytail, and a beard that is mostly grey. He's looking at me as

I'm looking at him. He's wearing a black T-shirt that says: Pig Iron Motorcycles – Fargo N.D.

'Pig Iron?' I ask.

He looks down at his chest, reading what is printed there. Does he not know which shirt he is wearing? 'It's a motorcycle shop,' he says. His voice has that bottom-of-a-barrel echo to it that big men get, but it's a pleasant enough voice. 'Harleys.' He looks embarrassed. 'Harley-Davidsons; they're a kind of motorcycle.'

'Yes,' I say, 'I know. My husband owned one. A 1927 Harley-Davidson.'

He smiles to himself. Here's an old lady making up stories, he's thinking. I can see him counting to himself, figuring things out. '1927?' he says.

'It wasn't new,' I tell him. 'I'm not that old, not quite. We owned it in 1943.' I look around the room, letting him think I'm bored with this conversation. 'I used to ride it a bit but I never really got the hang of the stick-shift.' Now he's taking me seriously. 'I understand they don't use them any more,' I say. 'Modern motorcycles are different.'

'No,' he says, 'they don't. Suicide shifts, we call them. And no, they don't use them any more.' He nods at the bamboo screen. 'Come in,' he says, gesturing with one of his huge and, now that I notice, very tattooed arms. 'Come in.'

It's like I've passed a job application, or the first obstacle on a treasure hunt. I follow him around the bamboo screen and into the back.

You learn early that people have expectations. I was a schoolteacher, before I married my husband. Of course it was before I married my husband: only single women were allowed to teach school in those days. Single women of good character. And one day the superintendent of schools had a chat with me. I was summoned to his office for a friendly little chat. He couldn't help noticing that my lights were on late at night. Sometimes very late at night, even midnight. Why, yes, I said, yes, that's so. I read a good deal, and sometimes.... It was expected that teachers of the children of our community do so with an alert mind and a rested body. The superintendent trusted that we'd have no more problems. We didn't. I sewed a thick set of curtains and did my reading in my kitchen, which didn't face the street.

The room reminds me, since I'm already thinking of one, of a kitchen. There's even a little half-fridge, tucked over in one corner. And, where I expected some sort of white-draped operating table or something, there is a red Arborite table. The table is ringed with chrome and is the sister of one that sat in my kitchen for over thirty years before I gave it to the Salvation Army people. Instead of a GE toaster tucked over at one end, though, there is some other sort of machine, but it is chrome and rounded, and would not look all that out of place in my kitchen. The man is fiddling with something over by the sink.

'I'm making tea, would you like some?' he asks. I notice now that he has a bit of an English accent. Yes, I tell him, that would be lovely.

'Camomile OK?'

Yes, fine, fine, I say. He pours water into a kettle while I look around. I'm standing there, looking at the posters on the walls, mostly naked women on large motorcycles, when he suddenly remembers to offer me a chair. I sit down, and neither of us mentions the posters. I am pleased that he isn't embarrassed on my account.

I find the tea quite refreshing. It tastes of mint, and I quite like it. I don't know if I'll stop drinking the Nabob, but I quite like this. I started with Nabob when they had coupons in the boxes and I've never switched. I don't think I ever bought anything with the coupons, come to think of it, but it's still a good tea. The secret is the pot, really.

'So,' the man says, 'what can I do for you, Mrs ...?'

'Prout,' I tell him. 'Evalyne Prout. And you are?'

He sips his tea, which he has in a large mug. He's given me an actual teacup. With a saucer, if you please. 'They call me the Dutchman,' he says. He looks slightly embarrassed, as much as a huge tattooed man wearing a black T-shirt can. 'But my name is Everett, Everett Smythe.'

'Well, I'm pleased to meet you Mr Smythe. But you don't sound Dutch to me, more like a Geordie.'

I've surprised him, as his eyebrows rise by a quarter of an inch. 'Newcastle-upon-Tyne,' he says, 'but that was a long time ago. You have a good ear, Mrs Prout.'

'Thank you, Mr Smythe, I suppose I do.' I look around the comfortable little kitchen area. 'You need a cat.'

He blows on his tea and then puts his mug down to look around, as if he expects to see one walk out from under the table. 'Yes,' he says, 'I suppose I do. But it's not allowed. They have strict rules for tattoo parlours. I'm not really supposed to make tea in this area.'

'No?' I say. 'Well, that would be a shame, wouldn't it?' And, the more I look around, the more the little space becomes a kitchen, the more we become two neighbours sharing a cup of tea in the afternoon.

When he makes another pot of tea he searches around for a bit and then presents me with a plate and two different sorts of biscuit. 'Just like an old-fashioned English at-home, Mr Smythe,' I say, and he looks pleased. The chime from the door rings and he gets up and goes into the other room. I follow him and stand in the doorway while he asks a young girl with dirty blond hair for some ID She complains, but he doesn't seem to hear her. She tugs down her T-shirt to show her left shoulder – I can see a flash of colour and that's all – but Mr Smythe shakes his head. Finally she leaves and we return to our tea and biscuits.

'How old were you when you got your first one?' I ask him.

He smiles and rubs at his forearm. 'This one,' he says, and rubs his thumb along a patch of faded blue. 'When I was in the Royal Navy. I was sixteen and did it myself.'

I lean forward and look more closely. It is, or was, an anchor, with some writing that I can't make out. The colour has faded to a grey-green and the lines have smudged. It doesn't look as if it was much to begin with. 'You've gotten better since then, I hope?'

He laughs. 'Yes, yes, I have. And now, Mrs Prout, what is it that I can do for you?'

I tell him that I am seventy-four years old and that I have been widowed for twenty-six years. I tell him that I have no children, and

I am increasingly frightened by loud noises, strangers, and change. My apartment smells of lavender and I don't know when I became old. I tell him it is my birthday.

'And now you want a tattoo,' he says.

'And now I want a tattoo,' I agree.

He nods his head and his grey beard rises up and down, up and down his chest. He reaches out and takes another biscuit. He eats it, delicate bite by delicate bite, without saying a word. I sit and watch him, and I don't say anything either. I wish that there were a cat for me to pet.

I tell him that my husband worked at a sawmill on False Creek. Any number of jobs whose names changed as he made five or ten cents more per hour, until he lost three fingers from his right hand to one of the saws. After that they made him what you call an oiler. He was the one who went around making sure all the machines were lubricated. Oiled. As far as I could tell that was the job they gave to someone they'd crippled but not quite killed. That's how it used to be. So I always had the thought in the back of my mind that he would go one day, victim of some kind of terrible and mechanical violence. When it turned out to be his heart it was almost a relief. He had insurance, after a fashion, and that was that. All of a sudden I was living alone in a sweltering apartment in Kerrisdale and people were giving me African violets. I look at Mr Smythe as if I expect him to understand all of this.

'Mrs Prout ...' he says. He has spread both his hands wide, their palms up, and is looking from one huge hand to the other. As if the words he were trying to find were carried in either the left or the right. 'Mrs Prout,' he says again, and I pick up my teacup, though I know full well that it is empty, and sip from it. I place it back on its saucer and stare him in the eye. 'Mr Smythe,' I say.

Mr Smythe sighs. He turns his hands over and grips the edge of the table, pushing himself to his feet. He clears away the cups and the plate and then stands looking down at me. 'Have you ever done this before?' he asks.

'Have I ever ...?'

'A tattoo, Mrs Prout. Have you had a tattoo done before?'

I look down at my arms, sticks covered in translucent skin and thin blue veins. Now it is I who am looking to find something. 'No, Mr Smythe, I have not.'

He sighs again. 'And now you've decided that you'd like one, as a sort of –'

'Birthday present,' I say, before he can. 'Yes, Mr Smythe, that is exactly what I would like. Do you think that you can do that for me? That is what you do, isn't it?'

He nods, his face stern behind his beard, under his hair, a pink dot in a cloud of grey. 'First I'm going to have to see some ID,' he says.

All the way home on the bus, I burn to touch it. I sit with my hands folded on my lap and I burn. I smile softly to myself and I wonder if people can tell. Would they say, should they notice, that something is different about me? Would they wonder what it is, what has this old lady done that makes her smile like this? A thin boy with messy hair stands beside my seat, and I see, stencilled into the pale skin of his upper arm, the cartoon of a young girl holding an ice cream cone. And I feel that we have a secret between us, we two, and he doesn't even know it. I smile, I beam at the boy, but he doesn't notice. It is enough that I know.

Looking over my shoulder into the mirror, I can see the gauze. Mr Smythe has told me to leave it on for three days, not to wash it, and then it may come off. My left shoulder blade is the location we finally decided upon, and I look at it now in the mirror. The gauze will come off but I still won't be able to see it, he's said. There will be a scab and I am not to touch it. I must wait until it comes off by itself, piece by piece. Bit by bit I will see what he has drawn on my skin. He has warned me that if I have second thoughts then, it will be too late. He has told me there will be no going back, and I have told him I will not want to. Still, he tells me this again, stresses the permanence of what I am about to do. I tell him I am ready. I tell him I feel as if I were seven years old, and it is early Christmas morning.

And, of course, I can't keep a secret. I had intended to, I truly had. My present to myself was to have been a surprise that I wouldn't see: when I am gone, and am being laid out, wouldn't everyone be surprised to see what was there, etched on my left shoulder blade. Who would have thought, I imagine them all saying, isn't that the strangest thing.

But, I find that I can't. I tell myself that I won't, as I am on the phone inviting my friend and neighbour Irene to come to tea. I tell myself that I can resist, as I am laying out the seed cakes and putting the water on to boil. And then the buzzer rings, and I know that I will tell all. And I am glad.

Irene spills her tea. Irene actually spills her tea when I tell her. 'Wait, wait,' she says. 'Start over, start from the very beginning. I want you to start from the very beginning.'

'Well,' I say, 'I decided – '

'Who would have thought? Who would have thought? Now start over, start right at the very beginning.'

'*Well,*' I say....

He wore pale yellow rubber gloves. The needles came out of a sealed package, I remember him using his teeth to tear a corner of it and thinking: that's probably not right. The needles fitted into a shiny steel appliance with a long black electrical cord. He plugged it into the same socket that he'd used for the kettle. He swabbed my shoulder blade with alcohol. I could smell it in the air, and my skin felt cool as it evaporated.

We'd decided that my shoulder would be the best. Mr Smythe told me that he's done them everywhere. Everywhere. He blushed when he said it, not something you'd expect him to do. I told him that my shoulder would be fine.

He drew the outline with a felt pen. He showed me the pen and it was like one a schoolchild might carry in her pencil-case. He told me that he draws free-hand and seemed quite proud of that fact. I hadn't really considered that there was any other way to do it.

The machine buzzed and vibrated, sounding for all the world like a neck massager I used to have. That I probably still have, somewhere. It stung, but not as much as you'd think. It hurt, but the hurt slowly moved as he carefully traced what he had drawn, and it wasn't so bad, not really. All in all, it wasn't so bad.

But what is it, what is it? Irene wants to know. I nibble at a corner of my seed cake, take a sip of my tea – how many cups have I had today, I wonder – and look Irene square in the face. 'I don't know,' I say.

'I beg your pardon?' says Irene.

'I don't know,' I say again. 'I let him choose.' I smile sweetly at Irene. 'I told Mr Smythe that I wanted to be surprised.'

Irene phones or drops by several times a day after that. 'Anything yet?' she asks, and I must tell her no, no, there is nothing yet. The gauze comes off, but there is still nothing to see. Even so, I pull the neck of my dress off my shoulder to show Irene. She leans in close, trying to see beneath the crust of dried brown blood.

'It's not very big,' she says.

'No, it's not,' I say. I too had expected it to be larger. I've decided that Mr Smythe must know best, though. He'd thought for a long time, when I asked him to do it. He'd tried to talk me out of it, giving me one reason after another, but I was resolute. So he must have made the right choice. Irene is burning with curiosity, and for some perverse reason this makes me act as if I were bored, completely bored with the whole affair.

'I suppose we'll know what it is, soon enough,' I say. And when Irene is gone I stand in front of my mirror trying to imagine what it is that is forever traced into my skin.

The doubts begin to come just when the scab is breaking away. What if it is something obscene? Worst of all, what if it is completely banal? What if, rather than the thing of tiny beauty I've imagined, it is clumsy and gross? What if, what if? I remind myself that I am a good judge of character, and that Mr Smythe would do no such thing. I tell myself that I have made my bed and now I will lie in it, no matter what shape it may be.

And still I worry, as I wait for the flakes of my dried blood to crumble and fall away. What was I thinking? When people find out, they will laugh at me. What was I thinking?

I was thinking that I wanted to do something and I did it. I was thinking that just because I've been one way for seventy-four years, day in and day out, doesn't mean that one spring day I can't be something else. I look at my reflection in the mirror, eye to eye with this face I have watched change, this hair that I've seen go from black to grey to blue, and I nod my head. I nod my head and I smile.

I almost miss my stop. I've been sitting, hands clasped together, staring into space, and when I look up I see that the bus has arrived. I see the Eaton's building and must struggle to get to the doors and down the steps before the bus leaves. It groans away, and I am left standing still on a sidewalk that is nothing but people hurrying from one place to another. I square my shoulders and begin to walk.

I walk right up to the door and open it. I hear the buzzing of his machine coming from the next room and I sit down. I don't read a magazine, I don't look at the posters and samples on the walls. I sit and I wait.

They are finished soon. I don't even notice the man who opens the front door and exits. I am waiting and watching to see Mr Smythe's face. 'Good day, Mr Smythe,' I say.

He nods when he sees me. Of all the things I'd imagined he'd do, this is not one of them. He nods, and then gestures with his arm. 'Hello, Mrs Prout. Won't you come in?'

He puts the water on to boil and then sets a plate of biscuits in front of me. 'You seemed to like these the last time,' he says. 'I bought some more.'

I glare at him, but he has turned back to fool with the teapot. 'No, thank you, Mr Smythe,' I say.

'Well, I'll just leave them there,' he says. 'Just in case.' And then he comes back and sits down at the table with me. He reaches and helps himself to a biscuit, eating it with tiny bites, afternoon tea with the Queen.

'You know why I am here, Mr Smythe?'

He nods again, his beard rising and falling on his T-shirt. This one is white and reads: Hog Heaven, Harleys Forever. I want to ask him if all of his clothing pertains to motorcycles, but I do not. I reach for a biscuit and then I pull my hand back. 'Mr Smythe –'

He stands suddenly. 'There's the kettle,' he says, though we both know it hasn't had time to boil. While he is fussing with the tea I eat a biscuit.

Finally he sits down again. 'Now, Mrs Prout,' he says.

'Yes, Mr Smythe. Now.'

And then we sit, neither of us saying a word. We sit long enough for the tea to steep, and Mr Smythe pours us each a cup.

'May I show you something, Mr Smythe?' I don't wait for an answer. I put down my teacup and undo the first two buttons of my dress. I pull the material down over my left shoulder and twist to show it to Mr Smythe. 'Tell me what you see, Mr Smythe.'

He is fidgeting, his big hands opening and closing. On one arm the tattoos end at the wrist, like the cuff of a red and blue patterned shirt. The other has the back of the hand thickly tattooed, though I can't tell what the pictures are. 'Mrs Prout,' he says, his hands moving.

I still hold the material of my dress down, and now I twist my head to look down at my shoulder blade. 'I'll tell you what I see, Mr Smythe, I don't see anything at all.'

'Mrs Prout.'

'I see nothing, Mr Smythe, just the fading outline of a cruel joke. Is that what you see? I'd like to know, Mr Smythe, is that what you see?'

When the scab first flaked away, bit by bit, and all I could see was the thin red outline, I thought that must be how it is. Maybe it takes a few days for the colour to come up, I thought. That must be how it is, and everyone knows it. Silly of me not to.

But once all the dried blood had peeled off, I was left with nothing but the thin outline of a teacup and saucer. I thought that quite sweet, a delicate teacup outlined in red. After a few days even that faded away. Until I was left with the faintest of ghost images, and the knowledge that I'd been had for a fool.

'Now, Mr Smythe, shall we try again?'

He takes a bite of his biscuit and then a sip from his mug of tea. When he smiles his teeth seem bigger and whiter than they should be. 'Whatever you say, Mrs Prout. Whatever you say.' And this time I watch him take up the little vials of ink, the ink that will make whatever he draws permanent.

He is just leaning in to begin work when he stops and pulls away.

'Mrs Prout,' he says, 'I'd like to make one thing clear.' I stare straight ahead, reading the neat labels on his tins of tea, coffee, sugar. 'What I did wasn't intended as a joke. It was –' I turn to look at him and I see that this is not easy for him. Good, I think to myself. He stands, holding his tattoo apparatus, not quite meeting my eye. 'I wanted you to be sure, Mrs Prout. I wanted you to have a second chance.' He's speaking in a strangely formal way, like a child in front of a principal or minister. 'I'm sorry if that hurt you. It was not intended to.' My eye has wandered, but now I study this bear of a man, his mass of hair and beard, his tattoos. I listen to his voice, the faint accent that he's carried with him despite all his changes.

'I understand, Everett,' I say, and I believe that I do. 'Please,' I add, 'you may call me Evalyne.'

When he is finished and the gauze is on, we wait for another pot of tea to brew, one that is properly made this time. He and I are the same in this, in our faith in tea, in the simple rituals of biscuits and good china for guests. And I smile to think that I have such a thing in common with such a man. Finally, when I can endure it no more, I ask him what he has drawn.

'Evalyne,' he says, 'you'll just have to wait.'

Steam

I'M GETTING TO BE THE AGE where I no longer know the price of anything. Let me give you an example. I'm out with some woman or other. We stop for tea and blueberry scones and before the bill is totalled up I have five dollars ready. More than enough, you'd think, including a good tip. Then the machine flashes $5.24 and I'm left to fumble around, searching for a loose quarter. And the woman I'm with, girl really, young enough to be my daughter if you fudge a year here or there, is watching me. A black leather mini, ankle socks trimmed with lace, little black fuck-me shoes, watching me search for a quarter. And afterward, of course, she wants to go drinking and dancing. And after that she'll want to come to my place, and I'll say we go to hers. I finish my tea but she doesn't touch hers, I don't think she knows what it is, and I tell her I have a headache. I give her fifty dollars for a cab or whatever and watch her walk away, black mini, one of those billowing six-hundred-dollar yellow leather jackets, long legs and all. Things change.

I go to a steam bath near my place. It's in a community centre, you know, on the up and up. Just so you don't get the wrong idea. Like a sauna but better. I go, and I sit in that steam, and I come out refreshed, at peace. It's remarkable.

I don't go all the time, you understand. I don't like to be predictable. I don't like people to know who I am, where I'll be. Maybe I'll tell you why sometime.

The steam bath, it's like a sauna. Wood. Benches. Fat guys sweating. The door's different, though. A sauna, it has a wooden door. The steam bath, it has a steel door, like an industrial fridge. To keep the steam in. There's a doohickey on the wall you pull, a valve, and more steam comes out. In a sauna, what you do is sit there until you're bored of watching sweat drip off the end of your nose. In the steam bath, you sit there until you think you're going to die. Then you sit some more. When I leave, after having a long cold shower, sometimes I stagger when I walk. You stay in the steam room long enough, you'll see God. And after that, I'm relaxed for days. I go maybe once, twice a week. And no, I never take anyone there. The steam bath is someplace I can be, someplace I can just be.

The thing with women is that, sooner or later, they want to start buying slipcovers for the furniture. Let them in the door and the next thing you know you're being told to keep your shoes off of the couch. Your couch. And then you're done for, my friend, and then you're done for. Two things I never do: let a woman into my apartment, or let her know my real last name. That sounds harsh, o k. But that's the way it is. We can go out, we can party, we can fuck, but it never happens at my place. Sooner or later they all start asking questions, of course, and it's time to say 'So long'. Which is a hell of a lot easier if they don't know your name or where you live, am I right? And, I'm getting to the point where I need them less and less. When I was younger, I'd wake up and think, 'If I don't get laid today, I'm going to die.' Now it's today, tomorrow, whenever. It's not the end of the world. You adjust. More than adjust, your priorities shift. Your needs change.

After I'd gone to the steam bath a few times, I saw that one guy was there more often than not. An older guy, maybe fifty or sixty, built like a bear. A big hairy chest and a huge, hard stomach. Not fat, but big. Looking like you could swing a baseball bat at him and it would bounce off. A big square head, and thick, furry eyebrows. I started thinking of him as 'the Russian' because he looked like that Russian leader, the one before Gorbachev. Brezhnev. Yeah, there were a couple of others in between there, but no one else can remember them, so why should I? He looked like Brezhnev. And Jesus, did he like it hot. It must be the Slavic blood or something. The first time I walked in on him I didn't think I'd make it to the bench. The air was so charged with steam that I had to hold my hands over my mouth just to breathe. He sat there, holding onto the valve and stuking the steam, soaking it all up. I lasted about two minutes and then I had to leave. The Russian. Jesus.

There's one thing I'd better get out front, right now, and then leave it alone. I don't want to have to keep coming back to it, going into all the details that everyone gets wrong from all the hysterical movies they've seen and novels they've read. I'm under control, I'm not turning into a werewolf or anything. I'm not out killing grandmothers for their television sets. I manage just fine, thank you very much. So that's all I have to say. I'm not going into all that needle-and-spoon bullshit. For the record: no one knows about it, I'm very careful and completely under control. I don't have lines of tracks up and down my arms, that's all movie hype. Some people smoke cigarettes, some people have a gambling jones, the horses or the stock market, what does it matter? Me, I have this. So that's that.

Except to explain that that's another reason why I don't let women come over. Or anybody. You can't be too careful.

You would never know. You'll have to believe me on this, but it's true. In the steam bath, naked, I can sit there and no one would ever know. I've got nothing to hide.

When I bought the gun, at first I didn't want any bullets. 'So why not use a banana, no bullets?' I was asked. I thought about it and finally, yeah, I took the things. So it's loaded, yes, but I would never fire it. Never. That's one of those things you have to think about, ahead of time. Philosophy, if you like. You make the hard decisions with a cool head so that when the time comes ...

You would be shocked how easy it is, and how cheap, to purchase a gun in this city. Better I should have it than some crazy kid. I wonder, sometimes, where it's all going. You have to wonder.

The Russian and I would nod when we saw each other. Usually he was there first, lost in the cloud of steam, his right hand pulling down on the steam valve. Only every now and again would I arrive before him, and then I'd be the one who sat in the corner, controlling the temperature. By this time I could bear it, at least survive. So I'd goose the heat, pulling down on the handle. The control was a rod sticking out of a hole in the wooden planks, and a chain attached it to a metal triangle that you pulled on. You'd think the metal would be too hot to touch, but it actually felt cool. Funny. And you'd also think, from having watched the Russian pull it down with one relaxed arm the size of my thigh, that it was easy. He'd pull the triangle all the way down and then sit there, roasting in the wet heat. With both hands I couldn't pull the thing down that far. Even so, I managed to get the place hot enough. Hot enough so that when the Russian came in he'd nod at me, and me at him, and then we'd sit, the only sound the hissing of the steam and the dripping of our sweat.

I don't go in for disguises – sunglasses, false beards, that sort of thing. Why not just wear a sign: Hey, look at me, I'm a Bank Robber. My face is different. It's hard to explain, but when you think of yourself differently, your face changes. So that's what I do. When I walk into a bank, I'm a different person. You'd never recognize me.

The Russian started bringing in this little bottle. Eucalyptus oil. The first time he held it up and showed it to me. There were three or four others in the steam, but they were just transients, you know? The Russian and I were the two regulars, so he asked me. Held up the little bottle, cocked his thick Brezhnev eyebrows, and asked 'OK?' He didn't sound like a Russian, of course. He sounded just like a regular guy.

I said sure, yeah, and he sprinkled a few drops out. The steam in my lungs turned into medicine, hot medicine. When you were sick, as a kid, did your mom have one of those vaporizer things? Vicks Vapor Rub. Maybe Vaporub, one word. When you were sick she'd spoon that stuff into a little steam machine, and the soothing steam would fix you right up, make you feel like you were living inside of something healthy. The eucalyptus smelled like that. I know what it is because I asked, and he passed the little bottle to me. 'Good,' I said, and he nodded. From then on, when I got there he'd pull out the little bottle, scatter a few drops. We'd nod at one another, smile.

And then he'd pull down on that chain, fill the room with scalding menthol steam.

Last year in Vancouver there were one hundred and seventy-three bank robberies. I did seventeen of them. The trick is not to be greedy. You have a monthly budget, you manage your expenses, you plan. It's like any job: you know pretty well what your income is going to be and you attempt to live within your means. And you do not get rich. My average take, averaged over the last five years, is four thousand two hundred dollars per job. That's tax free, of course, but you still see that it's not like on TV. I get by, and I keep my expenses steady, controlled. Of course I have a certain expense that I've already told you about, but I keep that steady, too. Pretty steady. I'll admit it can creep up on a person but it's nothing like you hear. People tell you stories: five hundred dollars a day, a week without sleep, ten thousand dollars in one jag. Sure, it can be done, but it doesn't have to be that way. With a little discretion and a little self-control, you'll have no problems.

What I like to do is go for a drink in a very fancy lounge. After, I mean. I walk away, turn a few corners, throw away the raincoat, re-comb my hair, and then go to the Four Seasons piano lounge for a six-dollar beer. Sit and listen to an elegant black gentleman play subdued jazz on the piano. I like that. I sit there, my attaché case beside my stool, just another businessman enjoying some afternoon jazz. The last time, I was leaning against the teak bar, watching the thick black fingers ripple up and down the keys, and the fellow next to me kept twiddling a cigarette back and forth between his fingers. He must have known that he was annoying the hell out of me because he grimaced and said, 'I'm trying to quit.'

'Oh,' I said. 'It must be tough.'

'Awful,' he said. 'You have no idea.' He wanted to talk more but I turned away. After a little more jazz and one more beer I took a cab home. I got out of the cab a block away from my apartment and walked. It's one of my private little jokes that I live downtown, in the business section. Near all the banks. What the hell, you might say I was taking a chance and you might be right, but I'd say I was having a bit of fun. And danger is always a part of fun, isn't it?

Spread out on the floor it didn't look like all that much, not measured in days and weeks. Six thousand five hundred dollars. That was three weeks ago and it's just about time again. It's just about time for me to go to work again.

I think both the Russian and I decided to wait the other out. It was the first time we arrived at the same time – I passed him in the changing room – and so we would be in the steam the same length of time. I think we both thought to ourselves, like kids do, 'Let's see how far this other guy will go. Let's see.' By the time he entered I'd managed to pull the lever all the way down. I made a discovery, then. You could wedge the metal triangle into the wooden slats so that it stayed there, all by itself, and the steam kept on and on. We sat, heads down, panting in the wet heat. Every now and then one of us would sit up, wipe sheets of sweat off of his chest, his face, arms. We sat and the steam hissed, filling the room with a deep scorching fog.

We quit at the same time. We both stood up, shaking our heads, throwing in the towel. After my shower, after I'd changed and was leaving, he walked beside me and slapped me on the back. I laughed and shook my head. He shook his, both of us laughing at the two dumb pricks in the steam room. 'See you,' he said. 'Take care.'

'Stay cool,' I said, and waved. I walked away and, waiting for the light to turn, saw him again a block away, tapping his attaché case against his leg, waiting for his light. He caught my eye, and we both shook our heads again, laughing.

I lied about the tracks. You always get tracks. But if you're careful, and smart, you get them in places that aren't obvious. So they're there, but even looking at them you wouldn't know what they are. I've probably lied about other things, as well. I'm in control of my life. I can do anything I want with it as long as I don't change it.

I waited patiently in line. I like Fridays. They're busy, everyone is bored and tired. And there's lots of money. So I stood, just another customer, moving my way forward place by place. That was always my favourite time, the waiting in line. You'd think it would be the moment with the most tension, the most fear. But in an odd way it was peaceful. As if I were in the right place, at just the right time, and only I know it. Everyone around me muttered and tapped their toes, impatient, but I was serene. Like a bridegroom in the hallway.

When I got to the teller I smiled and told her what I wanted. Never use a note, and never touch anything. I had to tell her again, I often do. People are never ready to hear that sort of thing, and their brains tell them: no, you misheard, listen again. So I told her again and she got that frozen, cat-in-the-headlights look they get, and then she slowly started taking money out of the drawer. They're well trained that way. And she was placing the bundles of bills in my attaché case, very carefully, very slowly, at great pains not to look at me, when I knew. Of course they have hidden alarms, but usually they're told not to touch them until we leave. But I knew. And I could hear the sounds in the bank change, so I knew something else, too. If I turned and looked I would see police cars approaching. So I knew that, too.

I took out my gun, and the metal was cold in my hand, and heavy. I thought of the metal triangle, the one in the steam room. I had time to imagine it completely. 'I'm going to leave, now,' I told the girl, and she said, 'Thank you.' She thanked me.

I turned, with the gun in front of me. I pulled back the hammer so that it was ready. I walked slowly, calmly. I was wrong about the police cars. I didn't see or hear anything. If I could get out the door and around the corner, maybe I could get away, I would be safe. I reached to push the door with my attaché case. I kept the gun pointed, ready to do whatever I had to do. And as I walked through the door I thought of the Russian. I thought of the Russian, hunched over on his wooden bench, looking up at me through his thick eyebrows, wondering if I could take any more steam.

True Confessions

'YOU FIND THAT PRETTY FUNNY, do you, Fowler?' Nils was saying. And he did, he found it hysterically funny. So then he knew enough to tell himself, You're drunk, Fowl, you're really drunk. Because usually there was nothing that Ted Sheldon could do that would pry even a smile from Fowler.

They'd been drinking retsina, it seemed like bottles and bottles of the icy turpentine, and Ted had done what was supposed to be a Greek dance – arms over his head, legs cancan-ing out in front – and then he'd picked up a paper plate, held it over his head, and smashed it to the floor. All of which, for some reason, Fowler found hysterical. So he was drunk. So sue him.

Besides, it was Ted's house and he could smash all the paper plates he wanted. And it was *meant* to be funny, wasn't it, so Fowler was just going along. He considered. Maybe Nils hadn't meant it as a reprimand, more of a way of joining in. Nils didn't drink, not more than a token polite sip from a glass that stayed full. And he hardly spoke, come to that. Fowler had known him for maybe twenty years, starting when they were in high school, and he couldn't remember having a conversation. Maybe Nils was just joining in, letting Fowler know that he was a regular guy. Fowler was thinking about this, trying to decide just exactly what was meant by what, when he noticed that Sheilagh, his wife, was talking to him, had probably been talking to him for a while.

'– aren't you, Fowler?' She was smiling. He blinked at her and ran his hands through his hair. And, yes, he grinned, because he was sober enough to know that he was terribly drunk and that everyone knew it.

'What was that, again?' he said.

'You're a good guy to be funny around. It's a good guest who laughs at his host's jokes.'

She reached over – she was sitting on the couch next to Nils and Fowler was in the armchair next to her – and shook his leg.

She smiled and he smiled back.

And, come to think of it, he wasn't the only one who'd had too much. None of them were drinkers, at least not any more. Consumption had fallen at a steady rate, year by year, bottles dropping away. Light beer and sparkling water had mostly replaced jugs of wine and twenty-sixers of hard stuff. So tonight was an exception, a surprise really, and he surely wasn't the only one caught by it.

Though Nils wasn't, of course. Nor was Mee-Ja, his wife. The two of them were a counterpoint to the others and always had been. Both were shy, he supposed that was how you would describe them, though Mee-Ja had a vivacity that Nils lacked. An effervescence. Fowler listened, hoping to hear her bubbling laugh – no, not bubbling, that wasn't the word. He tried to find the word that described the sound that Mee-Ja's laugh made him remember, but he couldn't do it. He'd have to stick with bubbling.

And now everyone was laughing and again he hadn't heard, had no idea why. Elizabeth raised her glass and, catching his eye over the brim, tipped the glass ever so slightly, toasting him. She took the smallest possible sip of her wine and continued to look at him. Her wry half-smile seemed to tell him that they shared something, something the others didn't know about, but he had no clue what it was. He looked away.

Fowler and Sheilagh had known Elizabeth the longest. Ted was her second husband, so he was a relative newcomer to the fold – only six years. Elizabeth and Sheilagh had been roommates or friends or something at university, before Fowler came along. And, something that Sheilagh didn't know, it was Elizabeth Fowler had spotted. She had an edgy beauty about her that drew your eye. She also had a cynical awareness of her sexuality, or so it had seemed to Fowler. There were complications within her, things that strongly attracted Fowler and then, almost simultaneously, made him think that her slightly less, slightly less *something* friend, Sheilagh, might be more his type. He emitted a small burp, redolent of garlic and raw onions from the Greek food that Ted had perfected during a month of Tuesday night cooking classes. He took a sip from his glass, but it was empty.

'Coffee,' announced Ted, hovering with a full glass pot. He must have been to the kitchen while Fowler was drifting. And, since there was already a tray of cups and spoons, cream and sugar, this was his second trip. Fowler put his glass aside. Enough was enough.

'It's caffeinated,' Ted warned, then began pouring. 'But I can make another pot if anyone would like.'

Fowler held out his cup. 'Throw caution to the wind,' he said, and the others laughed. He was pleased that his voice wasn't slurred, so there was hope for him yet. While everyone got fixed up they made the requisite small talk about drinking decaf now, about getting older, about the old days of double espressos and uninterrupted sleeps. Normally Fowler was the first off the mark, but now he sat and listened. Be more like Ted, he told himself, listen more, talk less. And almost immediately drifted off again, because who wanted to hear it all over once more. Like being trapped in amber, he decided, nothing changes.

He thought about names. Nils and Mee-Ja, a Dane and a Korean; a generation ago who would have thought that? But they were an almost ideal couple, or so it seemed. You can never tell, all you can go on is how things seem, but he supposed that everything was fine.

Ted and Elizabeth, Theodore and Elizabeth. Theodore had something to do with God, he knew. Nothing as simple as adoring God, but Theo, that meant God in Latin, he was pretty sure. While Elizabeth, she was the virgin queen. He laughed at that, chuckling to himself, but said nothing. He'd probably said it before. He'd probably said it many times on many evenings. Listen more and talk less.

He considered how many times in his life he'd explained his own name. Fowler. Though the explanation he gave was only half of one. A favourite of his father's, he'd say. A name that his father, an anglophile and himself the son of an immigrant from the Ukraine, had always liked. The other half, the half he never told though he was no longer consumed with embarrassment over it, was that it was the name of a book, a reference book that stood on his father's desk and in his father's heart instead of a Bible. *A Dictionary of Modern English Usage*, by H.W. Fowler. It was a miracle he hadn't been called Dick, he thought, and this time he laughed aloud.

Ted was talking. '"Every man should in his youth be a Socialist,"' he intoned, '"and in his maturity a Conservative." I forget who said it, but –'

'*You* said it, Ted,' Sheilagh said, and looked at Fowler over the rim of her coffee cup. Everyone was looking at him over their rims tonight. And then Sheilagh winked at him, winked at him before turning back to Ted. 'You *always* say it, but just saying something doesn't make it true, Ted, doesn't make it *history*.'

Fowler watched Ted fluff up under this riposte, a banty rooster with a cold wind up its backside. He loved the way Sheilagh accented her speech, used emphasis like a finger poking you in the chest. She didn't do it often – she let Ted or, yes, Fowler be the ones to pontificate – she just sat quietly back and occasionally stuck the shiv in. He loved that. And, looking at her now, sitting back with her slight smile, he loved her. A hell of a thing to be thinking. Sitting at a party after too much food and too much retsina, sipping coffee, listening to the conversation of close friends and what does he think about? How much he loves his wife.

His skull felt tight, and hot, as if a warm towel were being drawn snug. And his ears were buzzing, maybe that was one of the reasons he kept moving in and out of the conversation. Yes, he thought, he'd had much too much to drink. And, now that he was focused on his body, he learned that his bladder was full. 'Excuse me,' he mumbled and lurched to his feet.

He managed to navigate past the coffee table with no problems, so it looked as if he'd be OK. Then he misjudged the doorway by a fraction and bounced his right shoulder off the frame. Nothing serious, and he supposed no one noticed.

For some reason that had never been made clear to him, the bathroom was upstairs. The Sheldons had another one though, stranded in the middle of an unfinished basement. A white toilet and a basin, its copper pipes exposed, on display in the middle of the bare concrete room, enclosed only by open two-by-four framing. This was the bathroom that Fowler always used – he didn't think that Ted and Elizabeth approved, exactly, but to his mind he was in the right. The proper place for a bathroom was on the main floor and, finished or no, that was the one he would use.

And where do they get off calling it the basement, he thought. Still in the kitchen, he stopped dead at this and leaned against the refrigerator. What they called the basement was actually on the same level as the living room and the kitchen. The door to it led off the kitchen, no steps, same level, and yet they called it the basement. Funny thing. He pushed off from the fridge and sent a shower of plastic alphabet magnets to the floor. He walked across the linoleum, kicking letters as he went, who knew what words formed and then destroyed by his passage, and opened the door.

The smooth concrete floor reminded him of a skating rink in summer, something left over, out of place. Inside the jail cell that ringed the toilet, he leaned his head against a two-by-four as he urinated. Turning slightly, he watched the door to the kitchen, wondering if anyone would come through and see him. The loud splash of his urine echoed from the bare walls of the room, a huge sound, the piss of a giant. He finished up and then rinsed his hands under cold water. Usually there was an old towel hanging on a nail but tonight it was missing. He shook his hands, spraying drops of water, and walked through the empty frame doorway. In the corner of the room were the washer and dryer, each with a pile of laundry on top. He looked around, though of course he was alone, then walked over and pulled a towel from the mound on top of the dryer. He sniffed it to see if it was clean, couldn't tell, and wiped his hands anyway. Then he tucked it back under the rest of the heap.

The small pile on the washer was more interesting. Mostly Elizabeth's bras and panties, flimsy things in various shades of cream. He fingered the cup of a bra, rubbing it between his fingers, generating a heat from its thin silk. He picked up a pair of panties and then put them back, resisting the urge to stuff them into his pocket. Naughty boy, he told himself, speaking aloud, then turned and walked to the door.

In the kitchen he stepped on a letter, the hard plastic digging into the soft flesh of his instep. He swore, hopped on one foot, and caromed off the fridge. The last of the letters still stuck to the white metal crashed to the floor. Then, instead of going immediately into the living room, he moved to the sink. He ran a stream of cold water, cupping his hands to drink. It was as if he couldn't get enough, that nothing would finish off his thirst. Finally done, he didn't bother looking for a towel, just ran his wet hands through his hair, and headed for the living room.

No one had missed him. They were deep in discussion but it was all just words to Fowler. He sat down and thought about that. How conversation, when you're not part of it, ceases to exist. Becomes just words, sounds. Now Sheilagh reached out and touched his leg again. 'You OK, Fowl? Everything OK?'

He nodded. 'Sure. Fine.' Now he was talking in monosyllables, giving them even more cause for concern. 'I feel fine.' More monosyllables. 'Definitely.' And he had to smile at this, along with the others. Jesus, Fowler, you've really done it this time.

But when he sat back and thought about it, he realized that the others were in the same state, more or less. Not Nils and Mee-Ja, OK, but the others. Sheilagh was laughing at something Ted had said, her laugh just this side of hysterical. And Ted, always a bit of a showboat, was now in his glory. His voice was more, more orotund – there, Fowl, no more monosyllables – like he was on stage, performing for his audience. And Fowler felt a flush of affection for this frustrated hambone. Ted loved hearing their laughter, so what's so wrong with that. Fowler laughed along with the others, though he hadn't heard what Ted had said. He leaned in, blinked his eyes hard, and concentrated.

'The thing is, the thing is –' Ted was making himself convulse with laughter, he was crying and almost unable to speak he was laughing so hard. 'The thing is, that's what elephants are for!' He crowed with laughter, collapsing back on the sofa, while the others shrieked along with him. Fowler laughed dutifully, wondering if he'd missed too much. At least with Ted you knew when to laugh, you had all the signals. Like watching a sitcom on TV, everything was laid out for you. That's. What. Elephants. Are *for*! You couldn't miss it. He reached for his wine glass and then remembered that it was empty, that he wasn't going to drink any more.

Elizabeth was watching him again. He toasted her with his empty glass, then looked away. He tried hard to focus on the others' conversation, but now he couldn't distinguish words. All he could hear was the static of the individual voices, noise coming from different directions. He toyed with his glass, spinning it in his fingers, a prop. Not knowing what else to do with it, he put it down. There had always been something between him and Elizabeth, some kind of chemistry that neither had acted on. That both had consciously avoided, he thought. Or perhaps he had imagined it all. That was the thing, you could never tell.

Mee-Ja was talking now, her voice almost inaudible. Fowler, like the rest, had to lean in to hear what she was saying. A trick Ted should learn, he thought. The way to get people to listen is to say less, and say it quietly. Make them work for it. He rubbed his fingers together, feeling again the material of Elizabeth's bra. Smooth and rough at the same time. Was she wearing one like that, tonight? He sat back and rolled his head, peeking at Elizabeth. She smiled slightly, but didn't meet his eye. Had she seen him? Could anyone tell the ridiculous things he was thinking?

She was wearing a loose silk blouse, open at the throat. He couldn't tell if there was a bra under there, perhaps not. He stared at the blouse, wondering about the material, how it would feel smooth in one direction, prickly in the other as you stroked it.

Her skirt was long, below the knee, and made of some similar material to her blouse. Elizabeth knew how to dress, how to reveal and obscure her body to maximum effect. It was that line between showing and hiding that Fowler found most exciting. Peekaboo. Peekaboo.

He stood up and bumped against the coffee table. 'Think I'll get a drink of water,' he said, and edged his way past the chairs and legs. He made it to the kitchen OK, and walked over to the sink. He spun the faucet for the cold water and then stood there, leaning against the counter. He made himself breathe deeply, forcing air out, gulping it back in, willing his body to expel alcohol. He had to search to find a glass, opening and shutting cupboard doors, the doors on some kind of spring so they slapped against their frames when they closed. He discovered the coffee mugs and took one, a cartoon cat printed on the white ceramic, and filled it. He drank half the mug, refilled it, then gulped all of the water down. He refilled it again and turned the tap off, quieting the noise of the water. Still leaning against the counter with one hand, he drained the mug again, but slowly this time, drinking then pausing, drinking then pausing. He finished it and had just put the mug in the sink when he felt a hand on his shoulder.

'I wanted to make sure you were OK,' Elizabeth said. She left her hand where it was, so that Fowler spun under it, a dancer turning to face his partner.

He looked directly into her eyes and told himself that he wouldn't be the one to look away first. 'I'm fine,' he said. Already he felt the pressure of their mutual stare; for all the talk of looking into eyes, how much of it actually went on? He reached and brushed a strand of hair from her face and then, what the hell, cupped the side of her throat in his hand. Her skin was warm. 'I just thought that –'

Her tongue in his mouth was cool and small. He pulled her close and felt the heat of her body through the thin material. His right hand still on her neck, he ran his left down her arm and stroked her breast. He did it once, watching himself do it, a spectator at an accident, and then again. He drew the backs of his fingers across the warm silk, then flipped his hands and traced with the lightest possible touch of the pads of his fingers. A rough piece of skin on one finger snagged the material and then let go. Elizabeth now had her arms around his neck, and he dropped his hand from her throat to put it around her waist. Elizabeth traced a finger down his chest and belly and then, Jesus God, slid her fingers, the slightest tips of her fingers, under the belt and waist-band of his pants. Fowler gasped and Elizabeth pushed away. She brushed her blouse flat, again looking directly into his eyes, turned and left the room. He couldn't tell if she managed a straight line or not. He refilled his mug of water and followed along behind her.

Seated again, he found that the scene seemed a little clearer. The water helped. Suddenly he felt completely sober, if slightly removed from everything around him. And, as sober as he had become, the others had become inebriated. Even Mee-Ja and Nils seemed caught up in it all, Nils slapping his thigh as he bellowed with laughter, Mee-Ja telling some long and complicated story, waving her hands when she emphasized something.

He sipped his water. He looked at Sheilagh, who was intent on what Mee-Ja was saying, then reached and squeezed her knee. A little knee squeeze, just to let her know.

But what he was thinking about was Elizabeth. Elizabeth in the kitchen, the feel of her breast through silk, the cold shock of her finger tips just barely below his belt-line. He crossed then recrossed his legs, aware now that he had an erection. Likely he'd had it since the kitchen, and he hoped no one had noticed. Or almost no one, he thought, then tried to scrub from his mind, ashamed.

He wondered if he had to go to the bathroom again. His penis burned, he could feel the urethra like a hot cord through its centre. This must be what gonorrhea feels like, he thought. Maybe it was just that he had to urinate again, but he couldn't, not so soon. He'd given the others enough to talk about already. He recrossed his legs and rested his left arm on his thigh, camouflage.

He watched Ted, now silent. More than silent, he seemed to have lapsed into a coma. His eyes were open. but with heavy lids, and the half-full wine glass that he still held looked in danger of crashing to the floor. What's happened to us, thought Fowler. We're like a roomful of teenagers, drinking to the point of being sick.

Synchronous with this thought Ted burped, the sour garlic smell rolling over to Fowler, then swallowed several times in succession. Fowler took a sip of water. He suddenly felt compelled to swallow, to keep everything down. Please, God, don't let me be ill.

Sheilagh and Mee-Ja were trying to get their attention. 'Listen up,' Sheilagh said, bright eyed. 'Mee-Ja has a game we can play.'

Mee-Ja giggled. 'Sheilagh's idea,' she said, 'this is all Sheilagh's idea.' She and Sheilagh exchanged a glance and then both burst into laughter.

'*Our* idea,' Sheilagh said. 'It's true confessions time. What's the worst thing you've ever done? Share your guilt with your friends.' She looked around. 'Fowler, why don't you start?'

Fowler recalled that he'd played this game before, but couldn't remember where. Overdue library books and lying in court about a speeding ticket. 'Pass,' he said. 'My hands are clean.' He held out his hands, palms up, to show the room. 'See?' Elizabeth's nipple, just there, the tip of that finger there.

'I'll start,' said Sheilagh. 'I'll break the ice.' She paused, staring off into space feigning deep thought. 'One of the worst things I've done –'

'*The* worst thing,' interrupted Nils. 'You said we should tell *the* worst thing.'

Sheilagh nodded, sipping at her wine. 'OK, OK. But then the next person has to come up with something better. You have to out-terrible the last person who spoke, OK?'

Jesus, thought Fowler, what will it take? I killed six million Jews? In 1978 I forgot to leave the lid down on the toilet seat? Why are we doing this?

Sheilagh cleared her throat. 'Last year I backed our car into a car in the parking lot, and then I drove off.' She looked around, pleased with herself.

Fowler blinked. 'You told me that someone ran into *you*.'

Sheilagh held her hands up in triumph. '*And* I lied to my husband about it.' Mee-Ja cheered and Nils clapped his hands. Ted hadn't moved and, when Fowler looked at her, Elizabeth was swirling the wine in her glass, staring into the yellow liquid. She didn't seem a part of the same room.

Mee-Ja told a long story about cheating on an exam in university. Well, not cheating exactly, but there was something to do with a take-home essay and.... The details escaped Fowler and he allowed his attention to draw back, his thoughts moving into himself until the conversation in the room returned to the indistinct buzz that it had been. He watched Mee-Ja, her mouth moving, her face expressive. She used her hands for emphasis, stabbing at details, underlining themes. She seemed very happy, and Fowler wondered what it was about this game, about human nature, that made us proud and ashamed at the same time. Trying so hard to be bad, just to fit in. Good little players. He leaned over the coffee table, refilled his glass with retsina, and sat back.

Ted was awake again. And now he announced, in a voice that was sloppy with wine, a voice Fowler hoped he didn't share, that he wanted to play. He had a good one for everyone to hear.

Fowler watched the others, saw a quick twitch of apprehension cross their faces. Elizabeth, he saw, watched Ted intently, while Nils and Mee-Ja, Sheilagh, all looked away. What if Ted were drunk enough to really play the game, they might be thinking. What if he crosses that line, the one we're not quite sure of but know instantly when it is crossed?

But with his first sentence the room relaxed. Everything was OK,

Ted's story would fit nicely into the pattern that was established.

'When I was a teenager, maybe early twenties,' he said, 'I was at a party. All old friends, a party of old friends.' He paused and stared off into space, as if looking for the right words. Even blind drunk he knows how to play a room, thought Fowler.

'And there was this one guy no one liked.' Again he paused. 'No, that's not right. It's not that we didn't like him – he wasn't mean, or bad, just boring.' And again he paused, going too far, Fowler thought, being typical Ted and pushing too much of a good thing. 'So the party broke up early. We all hopped in our cars and then everyone, everyone except the one guy we didn't like, drove around the block and started the party again. Without him. And now I can't even remember who it was. Wasn't that awful?'

I should tell him it was me, thought Fowler. See his face. He drank from his retsina, not tasting the wine, drinking just a reflex, something you do at a party. Knowing Ted it had probably happened to him and all he'd done was change the names. Anything for a story, anything for a laugh.

But, whatever Fowler thought of Ted's performance, it certainly broke the ice. The others now fairly bounced in their seats, queueing for position. Each wanted a turn, they all wanted to show just how awful they'd been. You could practically feel the energy that charged the room. The sexual thrill of confession. Even Nils, stolid and reliably decent old Nils, was squirming in his seat. 'Well,' he kept saying, trying for an opening, 'well....'

Fowler stood up. Then, finding himself on his feet, he decided he needed to urinate again. Something to get him out of the room, something to give him a breath of air. He lurched against the coffee table and then was past. A glass might have toppled with his passing, but he wasn't sure. All he could see was the path in front of him. Only by concentrating completely on walking to the kitchen, away from the crush of these people, could he make it. The roaring in his ears was back, obscuring all other sound.

In the kitchen, he leaned over the sink, staring without focus into the burnished stainless steel. He discovered that he was panting like a dog.

A hand touched him on the waist and he jumped forward in

surprise, crashing into the counter. 'Are you all right, Fowler?' Elizabeth asked.

He turned around. Elizabeth stood appraising him, concerned. 'You don't look very well, Fowler. Are you going to make it?'

He leaned back against the counter. 'Sure,' he said, finding his voice, 'I'll be fine.' He thought about it. 'I think I've had too much to drink.' Now his voice in his ears sounded like Ted's. The mark of a drunk: trying to convince you that he knows he's drunk.

Elizabeth laughed. She kept laughing and reached out to him for support, her arm on his shoulder almost an embrace. 'God, me too, Fowl, me too.' She looked straight into his eyes, holding him. 'What the hell has happened tonight? We're dropping like flies.'

'The others?' Fowler asked, flicking his eyes toward the doorway and then back on Elizabeth. And now she looked away, glancing at the door as if she could see through into the living room.

'They're still at it, still baring their respective breasts to the room. Except Ted is having another snooze.' She shook her head. 'What's got into everybody tonight?' She stepped back from Fowler. 'I'm going to make another pot of coffee. Maybe that will help, I don't know.'

Fowler felt that he should say something, make what was happening a conversation, but he couldn't. Instead he leaned back against the counter, crossed his arms, and stared at Elizabeth. She returned the stare for several seconds and then abruptly turned away. She walked across the kitchen, but seemed to have forgotten the coffee machine. She reached and turned the handle of the door that led to the basement.

'I think I'll use your bathroom if you don't mind, Fowler.' She smiled at him and then disappeared through the doorway. The door swung back behind her but didn't close. Fowler continued leaning against the counter, studying the gap between the painted wood of the door and its matching frame. Elizabeth hadn't turned the light on, and the gap was nothing but black space.

He moved over and stood by the door. He cocked his head slightly, listening, wondering if he would hear anything. After a long time he heard her, or thought he did, the sibilant hiss of her urine echoing from the blank walls. And he could imagine her, sitting in the middle of the empty room, calmly staring ahead at the door he now stood behind. The roar of the flushing toilet moved him outside of his own body and he watched himself push open the door and walk through.

Elizabeth stood motionless in the middle of the room. He pushed the door shut, heard it latch, and moved to her. She pulled his face to hers, spearing his mouth with her tongue, his head held between her hands. He ran his hands up from her waist, groping at her breasts, his hands clumsy this time, and Elizabeth made the slightest of moans.

They moved together away from the centre of the room, one body with four legs, Fowler now with his mouth on Elizabeth's neck. They bumped into the dryer and it boomed hollowly in the dark.

Frantic now, Fowler slid his hand down the neck of Elizabeth's blouse. Under the silk, under the tighter silk of her brassiere, feeling for the hot swell of her nipple. Elizabeth was kissing his neck, biting it, attacking it with kisses.

She ran a fingernail down his chest and again stroked him just below the line of his belt. Then she reached lower, rubbing where his erection pressed hard against the front of his pants. She reached lower yet, cupping his balls, and then back up, the touch of her hand too hard, uncomfortable.

Fowler pulled at the silk of her skirt and ran his hand up her thigh. He stroked between her legs, feeling nothing but stocking and panties. He wormed a finger in the top of her panties, tugging slightly, trying to pull down. At the same time Elizabeth fumbled with his belt, attempting unsuccessfully to release it with one hand.

Then, together, they leaned apart. Fowler unhooked his belt, pulling it free from the loops, and lowered his zipper. Elizabeth pulled her panties and panty-hose down. Fowler saw that she stepped only one leg out, leaving the other with bunched panty and stocking at its ankle, a tail to drag along behind.

They pressed together again, Fowler's tongue in Elizabeth's mouth, his eyes closed. She tugged at his underwear and then grasped his erection in her hand. Fowler opened his eyes then, and found himself staring down at the pile of laundry that was heaped on top of the dryer.

He couldn't tell if he was inside her when he came. He hoped so, but likely not. He came almost instantly, in her hand, on her thighs, down the front of her watered silk skirt. And then he froze, paralysed, and Elizabeth frozen with him.

'Oh, shit,' she said finally, and dodged out from underneath him. He leaned over the dryer, his hands wrapped in tangles of towels and Ted's boxer shorts. He heard water running from the sink in the middle of the room, but didn't turn around. He continued to stare at the laundry, his breath coming in gasps, and then the door to the kitchen opened and closed again, Elizabeth gone. A slight breeze squeezed through the doorway and reminded him that he was standing in the middle of a empty basement with his pants bunched at his feet.

He wiped himself with a towel, smearing it with cold and gluey gobs of his semen. He pushed the towel deep into the pile on top of the dryer and pulled up his pants. He walked over to the toilet and urinated, his penis half-erect in his hand. He washed his hands in the basin, then combed his hair with them.

The kitchen was empty. He started for the doorway and then, remembering the plastic letters that littered the floor, got down on his knees. Sweeping with his hands and forearms he managed to gather them together in a pile in front of the fridge. He half considered leaving some kind of message with them, then merely stuck them to the white enamel, a jumble of possibilities.

The roaring in his ears was back. He could hear his friends talking but the voices blurred into the roar, the words obscured. Even when he went into the living room and sat down, he couldn't tell what they were saying.

Everyone was there, even Elizabeth who neither caught nor avoided his eye. She was, he saw, still wearing the same skirt, though she must have cleaned up. Sheilagh put her hand on his knee and he jumped, though just a little. And now everyone was looking at him, some faces concerned, some amused. And, like a radio suddenly coming into tune, the roaring in his ears faded and he could once more hear what people were saying.

'Look,' they said, 'look at Fowler.' The faces leaned in closer. 'Are you all right, Fowler buddy?'

He took Sheilagh's hand in both of his and held tight. He opened and closed his mouth, unable to think of the right thing to say. Finally, he raised Sheilagh's hand to his mouth and kissed her fingers. 'I'm fine,' he said, 'I'm OK.'

Which seemed to mostly satisfy them. And it was mostly true, at that. Except now he had to decide what to do. He thought about that, about what the right thing would be. About how, no matter what he decided, it wouldn't be completely right. Sheilagh squeezed his hand again. She wasn't looking at him, didn't want anything, she was just squeezing his hand, a little squeeze. And he knew then that, no matter what, he would have to tell her. Because there are rules and consequences to every game, even if you don't know them before you start.

Foncie

HELEN AND RICHARD SIT WAITING for their son, Mark. The restaurant is the same as the last time, almost eight months ago, and they'll likely choose it again their next trip to Vancouver. They both grew up here but neither has lived in the city for thirty years, and it's no longer home. This is Mark's city now. He was the one who picked the restaurant the first time, in desperation since neither Helen nor Richard could choose, each saying, 'Oh, it doesn't matter, whatever *you* like,' until he was ready to scream. The restaurant is popular with people Mark's age, or younger, but sufficiently expensive that Richard and Helen can feel that they're offering him a treat. Lord knows, he probably doesn't have much money.

Richard toys with his beer, Helen with her poisonous wine 'cooler'. Once, when you ordered that you got a tall glass, ice cubes with soda water and lemon, and a cheap, dry Italian white. Marketing has taken over, however, and what sits in front of her is a green bottle topped with pink foil, a product of the Canadian petrochemical industry. She will have to remember. But for now they each need something to tinker with, a focus, while they wait for their son. Richard, Helen knows, longs for his paper; and she, if truth be known, would prefer to finish the novel she carries in her purse, but she has a horror of becoming two strangers reading at the same table. Not us, she thinks, not yet.

Finally, Richard speaks. 'That wasn't too bad, was it?'

Helen shakes her head. 'No,' she says. 'But not good, either.' They are now of the age where they go to funerals. In the last few years it seems that the number is doubling, then redoubling. Odd, when you still consider yourself young, or at least not old, to have friends who have come to the end of their lives.

This last one was a shock. Unlike most of the others, Susie, Susie Leung, Susan Ng for the last thirty-five years – the shadows and details one must keep adding to memories – was exactly their age, was exactly like them. Richard and Bill, Susie's boyfriend, then husband, had been close friends. Susie and Helen, first classmates at university, then finding themselves to be girlfriends of best friends, soon became likewise. In those days that was how it worked. The women went with the men, adapted to their friends, their environment. Helen wonders if things have changed in thirty years. She doubts it.

Susie died at work. She still worked, though she had been planning to retire at the end of the year. Insult to injury, it seems to Helen, not just not making it to retirement, but actually to go at work. What was the last thing she saw, the staff room at Bing Senior Secondary? A notice requesting that all teachers please have their curriculum plans in by next Monday? They found a mountain of papers, essays, tests, lesson outlines on her desk. At least she didn't go in front of a class, explaining for the twenty-ninth class who Radisson and Groseilliers were. Radishes and Gooseberries. They all thought she was asleep and no one bothered her until she didn't show up for her 1:05 class. Heart. The doctor said there was no pain, but they always say that and how can they know?

Helen remembers Susie, while they were still in university. They'd all gone out somewhere and someone they met, she couldn't remember who, leaned towards Susie and said, 'Excuse me, I hope you don't mind me asking, but where are you from?'

Susie smiled warmly at her, Helen thinks. 'Vancouver,' she said.

The person, a woman Helen is almost sure – she can almost see her face – was annoyed. 'No, you know what I mean, where are you *really* from?'

Susie leaned towards the woman and whispered, conspiratorially. 'Well, I'm actually from –' and here she lowered her voice even more, drawing the woman closer, '*North* Vancouver.'

'Iris MacIntosh.'

Richard raises his eyebrows, and Helen realizes that she has muttered the name aloud, even as it came to her.

'Oh, I've just put a name to a face, that's all.' Would Iris MacIntosh remember saying those things? Probably not, thinks Helen, but that was the face that had finally formed. Iris MacIntosh. She would likely have no memory at all of saying that, and yet Helen is now sure. Memories are funny things, edited, re-edited, filed away. Has she said or done things that lived on in others' memories, things that she would now swear never happened? Lots, probably.

And where, thirty years later, would Iris MacIntosh be? So many faces.

Richard, too, is thinking of Susie. Thinking about the times, really only one or two years, when the four of them were close. They were younger then than Mark is now, he thinks, shocked. Somehow, in his memories he is always the same age, always possessing the same abilities, the same personality. Was he like Mark, then? A better question would be: is Mark now like he was? Richard looks out the window, moderately annoyed that Mark is late. Probably yes, probably no. Every memory is filtered by time, tinted by experience. Mark doesn't remind him of himself as much as he reminds himself of Mark.

Mark. His son is twenty-seven years old, four and a half units short of a university degree that has been on again, off again for ten years, living in a shared house, considering becoming (in no particular order) a painter, a bass player, a welder, several other things that Richard can no longer recall, and, finally, a stand-up comic. Stand-up comic is the latest, at least so far. If Mark phoned up and announced that he had become a Hare Krishna and was now selling daisies at the airport, Richard would just nod and ask if he needed to borrow money. Their friends, too, have accepted a certain different set of realities for Mark. They seem genuinely interested in what he does, what expected thing he is *not* doing. Behaviour that from their own children would cause them hysterics, coming from Mark brings only slow noddings of heads, wistful comments about how *they* had always wanted to shave their heads, to sell daisies. Richard knows what they mean, but it doesn't stop him from worrying about his son.

Or hating Vancouver, for that matter. Is it the fact that everything has changed that bothers him? What, for example, used to be where this restaurant is now? The memory is like a throbbing tooth – he can almost make out the building, but then it fades. He is now used to a smaller town, of course. The traffic noise drives him crazy. The crushes of people. And all the insider knowledge that he has long forgotten – the only way to go left off Burrard during rush hour is to first go right; this street becomes one way, that has a traffic barricade at the end of the next block; don't begin driving when the light turns green or you'll surely be killed by the three cars running the red light the other way. Perhaps he once knew all these things, but now they just make him uncomfortable, an outsider. Vancouver is no longer home, hasn't been for a long time. It is where his son lives.

Mark arrives, out of breath. He kisses his mother and shakes hands with his dad as he half rises. 'So, how are things?'

This question, and 'What's new?' are the basis of all their conversations, now. They know each other too well to make small talk like strangers, and yet they are so far removed for such long periods that intimate discussion is no longer possible, or even a consideration. Mark orders a beer, so now he too will have something to toy with.

Mark has come to the restaurant by bus. For some reason it was extremely crowded, and he had to stand, holding the overhead rail, looking out the window, while bodies and backpacks and umbrellas poked him in the back and sides. Perhaps he would find something that he could use in his act tonight.

His act. He smiles at the term. He is very careful never to phrase it that way to any friends. With luck, one day it will be an act, today it is – well, he can't say.

Tonight is 'Amateur Night', which means the same group of seven or eight would-be comics, honing their material. Of the seven, perhaps three are genuinely funny. The rest recite the same routines, painfully belabouring the same dull material over and over. Mark can sit backstage and mouth, word for word, each of their acts. He hopes that when it is his turn, sweating, staring into the light, feeling time somehow both speed up and slow down, that no one is behind the curtain, mouthing his words.

The would-be comics get to drink their beer at staff prices, know the club owner by his first name, and the promise of perhaps doing a tour of the bars of northern B.C., one day. Mark loves it.

He orders, as usual, an enormous steak. Except for the one or two times a year that his parents might be in town, he never sees meat. Or at least not meat that hasn't been ground, freezer burned, discounted, and then turned into either chili or any number of mutations of spaghetti sauce. Besides, his father is pleased, twice a year, to provide. Almost as if it were Mark doing him the favour.

Richard orders the same steak as Mark, and a carafe of house wine as well. Again his memory does funny things to him. It isn't that he is surprised by the prices of a meal, but, somewhere in the back of his brain, forever engraved, are prices, expectations from when he was Mark's age. To reconcile those hazy memories with what will be an eighty-dollar meal for three people, well, sometimes that is hard. Another sign that he is getting old. His father felt the same way, he supposes. He refused to eat corn and never failed to shake his head in wonder that Richard and Helen would pay good money for 'animal food'.

Richard reaches for the salt, sees Mark look at him, and replaces it. 'Maybe not,' he says, 'bad for the heart.' Mark smiles at him. Jesus, Richard thinks, first I get it from my father, then I get it from my son. When will it be my turn to know all the answers?

Helen eats a bite of a prawn and watches the waitress walk away, turning into Susie Leung. Susie, who became Susan Ng, who became Vice-Principal Ng, who got a card each Christmas and per- haps a letter every year or two, and who was buried at two o'clock that afternoon.

Mark is arguing with his father about politics. By means of some internal clock that they share, each year or two they switch positions. Suddenly each espouses beliefs that only a year ago, likely at the same table in the same restaurant, he ridiculed coming from the mouth of the other. This time Mark is apolitical, arguing that all pol- iticians are corrupt, that all that any party seeks is to gain power and, once it has achieved that, to retain it.

Richard, echoing the Mark of only a few months ago, is beside himself, demanding to know how Mark can compare ...

Helen wishes she had a tape recorder. They could just replay the tape, in a year's time, and then each could argue with himself. First they would have to listen, she thinks. Two peas in a very familiar pod. She looks out the window.

There was a man, she remembers, who used to take your picture on Granville Street. A street photographer. You'd be walking down

Granville, at night she thought, but couldn't be sure, and he would take your picture. He had a silver trunk, or stand, on wheels, and that was his camera. You'd be walking to a movie, or on your way to get a drink or a hamburger, and he'd take your picture. He was smart and looked for couples, or pairs of couples. FLASH, would go the camera, and you hadn't even noticed him yet.

'There! That's a nice picture. Let — take you a memory. When will this night come again, eh? It's almost tomorrow; let — take your picture.'

The patter was quick, without a pause, not giving you a chance to refuse. She thinks that he had an accent. The first picture was just the flash, of course. To get your attention. And to make you feel that he'd already given you something, for free. It would be rude not to stop. In those days you didn't brush by someone who talked to you on the street; you didn't avoid the eyes of anyone not moving on the sidewalk.

Had they bought a photograph? You paid him, and he wrote down your address, and the picture arrived in the mail. No Polaroids, not then. Had they done it? Paid the twenty-five cents, or dollar, or five dollars, and had him take another picture, a real one, and then mail it to them? Was there, somewhere, a faded and grainy picture taken by — of Susie and Bill, and Richard and her? Where would that picture be now? The photographer was at least middle-aged then, to them he looked ancient, and would surely be dead now. And his silver case, his camera, where would it be? Foncie. She remembers now. His name was Foncie.

Over dessert, Richard and Mark argue about the U.S. invading Canada. Or, rather, they are arguing about what would happen after that; both seem to agree that it would happen, should Canada do something provocative: like elect an NDP government. The waitress comes by with refills of coffee, and Helen watches Mark watch her walk away; she is amused to see that he is likely totally unaware that he does it, not even pausing in his conversation. Richard, she notices, doesn't even register that she was there, so wrapped up is he in his argument. When does a man stop noticing, she wonders. Perhaps Richard has never noticed? She smiles; no, that's unfair.

Richard is advocating guerrilla war. Richard, her fifty-eight-

year-old husband, who no longer notices twenty-year-olds in min-
iskirts, is going to take to the woods with a deer rifle.

'Hit and run,' he is saying, 'that's something no army can stand up
to. The Viet Cong won a war, fighting in black pyjamas. We could
do it too.'

Mark looks at his mother and winks. 'What, fight in our pyjamas?' Mark and his father have their own version of warfare: stylized
combat. She winks back, but Mark is already arguing in earnest.

'Look, Dad, it wouldn't be that simple. Who are you going to
fight, the Americans?'

'Of course the Americans. Or anybody else who invades Canada.
Sometimes you *do* need to defend yourself, at least on your own
ground.' Richard's voice is getting louder, a sign not just of wine but
that he is uncomfortable with what he is saying.

'And who do you fight when the Americans choose to support a
stooge government, one that invites them in? You still going to take
potshots at people when they're guys I grew up with, guys who are
just doing what every group of guys with guns is always doing: just
following orders? Who are you going to shoot then?'

And so on. Helen has long ago concluded that Richard and Mark
believe exactly the same things; they just don't know it yet. Their
arguments are more like internal debate, two halves trying to come
to a consensus. Meanwhile, the waitress has come with the bill; a
good point at which to announce a ceasefire. This time both Mark
and Richard watch her, careful to look three feet to the left of her so
that no one will suspect that they are watching. Again, Helen smiles.

The waitress leaves the bill on the table, smiles at Richard, and then
is gone, scanning the restaurant for whatever needs doing. A good
waitress lives in the future, thinks Richard, always looking ahead,
never doing in two trips what can be done in one. He watches her
go, noticing for the first time how short her skirt is, how long her
legs are. I could end my life, he thinks. One touch and the life I have
lived for thirty years would be over.

He turns back to the table and picks up the bill. Sometimes, in
stores or movie theatres, he has the same impulse. The impulse isn't
sexual, or at least he doesn't think so; he has it towards men and

women both, and the drive is similar to the one that makes him touch a hot stove, or lean out from a tall building. Contemplate shoplifting. Challenging death, he supposes. He feels rather silly, and busies himself with his charge card. Do other people have these thoughts, he wonders, and briefly prays: please don't let me make a fool of myself.

Helen and Richard are going to see Mark perform. All three of them are careful to appear blasé, as if this were no big deal. Helen did, in fact, ask at dinner if Mark would prefer them not to be there, but he said no, that was fine. He told them that the hardest step in anything, the one that means you are serious, is making your mistakes in public. Until you do, it doesn't count. No, he says, he'd like them to be there.

Richard asked, chuckling, if there was anything that he should warn them about. Mark shook his head. 'But you have to realize that it's not me up there. If I talk about my Mom and Dad, about my childhood, it's not you. It might sound like me, or be based on you, but it's different. Do you understand?' They told him that they understood. All memories are like that.

The first person on stage tells, in quick succession, three jokes about female genitalia. He then panics, increasing the velocity and crudity of each joke. He soon leaves the stage, his face pale. Helen, despite the material, feels sorry for him and claps; not long, and not hard, but she claps. Richard looks at her and she shrugs. 'Let's hope he does the same for Mark,' she says.

The next comedian, a stooped and pale man in his late thirties, with thin hair and beard, has obviously been here before. This must be one of the ones Mark told them about, Helen thinks. She watches in horror as the audience, in unison, chants the punch line to each of the man's jokes, seconds before he himself says them. Finally, when the punch line comes before he can even begin the joke (he doesn't even alter the order of his material, thinks Helen) he walks off stage without a word. The viciousness staggers her. Will he come back next week? Is that what it takes to succeed? She fears for Mark, more than she has in a long time.

Richard, after the first barrage of jokes from the first comedian, loses interest. I first heard those when I was Mark's age, he thinks. Younger. He sits, numb, amazed by what people find funny. Most of what he hears attempts to elicit laughter by shocking. Richard finds that he is not easily shocked, at least by this. He wonders if many people are, any more. He thinks back to when he was sixteen or seventeen and heard his father, having just crushed a thumbnail with a hammer blow, hiss the word 'fuck' under his breath. He'd never heard a parent use that word before, certainly not his father, and had almost believed that the boys of his generation (girls likewise never used that word) had invented it. Did my father pause, he wonders, between the blow landing and the word escaping, to consider if I was old enough, to decide that this was a good time? Did I ever do the same for Mark, one day let him know that I considered him an adult, an equal? Perhaps tonight they will find out if Mark considers *them* equals.

After a minute or two of watching the stage again, but not hearing, a funny thought occurs to him. What ever happened to that hammer?

Mark does not sit with his parents but hangs out backstage with the other regulars. He doesn't bother to watch the acts that precede him; they come back again and again but aren't regulars, not part of the in-group. Mark feels a tinge of shame that he, and all the rest, consider them losers, people not worthy of attention. But there is something about their failure that seems self-imposed, as if they were consciously responsible for their status, their lack of whatever the intangible is that matters so much. Mark, in fact, can no longer bear to listen to the opening acts. The desperation is too much, too embarrassing. He suspects the others feel this way too. It's enough to fear your own failure; it's unbearable when it's another's you have to watch and it reminds you of your own.

Instead, he drinks coffee and floats on the periphery of the inner circle. The nucleus is the club owner, himself a comedian, and any of the pros or semi-pros who are there watching. Success is a very relative thing, Mark realizes. They are not being paid to be here tonight and are not here to watch what they consider very inferior entertainment, but because this is the place where they have status. It's a family of sorts, with the same rigid hierarchy present in all families: the only difference is that it is mutable, fortunes rising and falling, faces appearing and disappearing based on one very simple variable: the amount of laughter produced. Despite this awareness, despite the desperation, this is where Mark wants to be.

The other would-bes, the other serious amateurs, are all Mark's friends. His only friends, really. His time now is spent either working on his act, practising and performing it, or watching others, hoping to learn. There's a chance that he'll get to go on the road soon, although this road only runs as far as outlying suburbs, perhaps four or five towns on Vancouver Island. Still, that would be work, professional work.

He goes on in a couple of minutes. He finishes his coffee and walks to the edge of the backstage, watching the drowning thrashings of the act on stage.

Out front, Helen and Richard clap with relief as the boy leaves the stage. After a moment the MC comes on and demands that they clap one more time. Even Richard applauds, a small enough thing to do for someone else's son. The MC announces the name that Mark uses, and Mark appears. Helen and Richard watch this adult, this almost stranger walk confidently to the microphone and remove it from its stand. He pulls up the tall stool that is the only prop on stage and then seems to change his mind. He walks toward the front of the stage.

'Hello,' he says, and quite a few people, Mark's friends, Helen thinks, laugh and 'hello' back. 'I'd like to welcome somebody to the club,' Mark says. 'Say hello to my mother and father.' And suddenly the applause is for them. Richard, his ears burning, at least knows what to do and gestures to Helen to half rise and wave to the rest of the audience. Mark beams at them, him now the proud parent, and they return to their seats.

'OK,' Mark says, 'thank you.' He reaches for the tall stool, half sits and half leans on it, and begins. And Helen and Richard sit there in the dark. Proud, fearful, full of love, hoping to laugh.

Cooties

CAROLINE IS TALKING. Roberta and William are over at Caroline and Peter's for dinner and Caroline is talking. She's telling them about her daughter, Beth, who is nine and perfect. At least she no longer asks when Roberta and William are going to have kids.

They're hearing about Beth and her school. Caroline is talking and Peter is replenishing wine glasses and the lamb is exquisite.

'Cooties, they call them,' Caroline says. 'And fleas, too. Somebody fleas, like Smith fleas, or Jones fleas, the whole family has them and no one will go near them. Isn't that something?' She takes a minuscule sip of her wine. 'Although I'm sure we did something much like it. Fleas, cooties. Children are beasts, really.' Even as a child, while they were growing up, Caroline sounded like what she is now, a forty-five-year-old woman. But she sounds like a forty-five-year-old Englishwoman. You'd expect her to talk about A-levels, and 'hols' and such, all in a plummy accent. Caroline, like Roberta, was born and raised in Saskatoon.

Caroline cuts a tiny morsel of lamb, brings it to her mouth, chews and swallows before speaking again. 'Complete beasts. I'm sure we were horrid when we were that age.' She laughs before taking another sip of wine. 'Still, I suppose there's no harm done. And she'll soon grow out of it. We did, didn't we, Roberta?' Roberta has a mouth full of salad at the moment and can only nod.

In retrospect, the rules must have been awfully complicated. Complicatedly awful, she thinks might be a better way to put it. If someone with cooties touches you, then you have them and she doesn't. Usually. Sometimes you both have them, but Roberta is unclear on the distinction. She recalls something about transmission at a distance, the concrete childhood version of guilt by association. If the infected person walks onto the grass, then you were expected to shriek and leap onto the sidewalk. If that person is touching the school, then you must not. Wherever they go, whatever they do.

'Who's for trifle?' Caroline asks. Roberta reminds herself to be tolerant. After all, Caroline does go to amazing lengths to entertain. And, come to think of it, it usually is Caroline and Peter who entertain. She and William do have them over, of course. Though it's infrequently, and certainly never for lamb, asparagus, new potatoes, summer squash, and trifle. And freshly ground coffee, thick cream, and liqueurs. And, and, and. Roberta offers to help serve up dessert, and tells herself, again, to 'be nice'. She didn't use to be like this, she thinks, always finding fault. She's intelligent enough to realize that the problem is likely hers, not Caroline's, but that doesn't change her mood. Knowing you're being a bitch doesn't mean a phony English accent and endless subtle references to how much money, in fact, your hosts possess won't still drive you up the wall. Be nice, be nice, be nice, Roberta thinks. I wasn't always like this, was I? When we were kids, was I this uncharitable, this judgemental? She wants to ask Caroline, but how do you phrase a question like that?

'Beth is one of the lucky ones, of course.' Caroline is back on Beth. Which is, truly, not surprising. Beth is a wonderful child and something of a fall harvest, after all. Caroline and Peter had her when Caroline was thirty-six, so who can really blame them? Until then Roberta thought that the two couples would each be childless. There seemed to be a symmetry; unfair to resent Caroline now because there no longer is.

The apple of their eye has, however, been banished for the evening. Caroline and Peter feel that children do not belong at dinner parties. Caroline tells Roberta that she can set out the serving and dessert spoons. Sterling, polished each Sunday by Peter.

'She's a bit of a leader, I think. So she is one of the mob shrieking about the poor outcast with the fleas. Cooties. Roberta, did we call them fleas or cooties? Do you remember?' She's standing there, absentmindedly licking some cream from a finger, looking at her. And she's no different from the woman she's always been, the girl she was before that. The friend Roberta has loved longest and best, despite everything.

'Both, I think. Maybe some other things as well.' Roberta isn't sure she wants to think about this any more. A homogenization takes place, over time, a gentle smoothing of the great joys and pains, and she isn't sure she wants to relive any of them. She isn't sure she wants to know what her role was in the daily battlefield of the playground. 'Kids and their games.' Caroline laughs and returns to spooning trifle, and Roberta smiles. Maybe she would remember better, understand more, if she had a daughter coming home each day, sometimes in tears, sometimes in triumph.

Back in the dining room over coffee and the trifle, the conversation, implausibly, continues. Peter and William examine the topic from various angles and disciplines. History and psychology. The nature and role of the scapegoat in ancient religion and modern boardroom. Someone mentions 'The Lottery', and it takes a few minutes to remember Shirley Jackson's name. Eventually Peter is reminded of a case his firm had something to do with, and he and William are off, sailing away into a male sunset that seems to be the same conversation, dinner after dinner. Do we sound like that to them, she wonders. After all, what really is the purpose of social conversation. Not knowledge, not really, information is the least of it. A social contract, more likely, an acknowledgement that you listen, each to the other, and that you value what is said. But you don't, not really; what you value is the saying. After a bit they move into the living room, and very shortly after that Peter takes William upstairs to see his new laptop. In the old days it would be shotguns, or model trains or something. Men seem to need an excuse, a focus. Their own company embarrasses them.

Caroline, impossibly, maddeningly, keeps worrying away at the same topic. It seems she's after something, or at least preoccupied. Perhaps she hasn't left her Saskatchewan school days as comfortably far behind as she ought. Roberta doesn't think that she herself has, either, and wishes she had gone to visit the laptop. In the old days, of course, the women would compare childbirths and do the cleaning up. Console one another over cracked nipples and husbands who expected more sex than was supposed to be required. Was it ever like that, or am I confabulating again, congratulating myself on how far I've come, we've come, she wonders. Caroline is talking and, with a smile and an implied wink, Roberta rises and pours them each a liqueur. Roberta has an Amaretto, from the bottle she knows is there especially for her, and she pours Caroline a small glass of Tia Maria.

She changed schools in grade 3, for reasons she can no longer remember. Perhaps they'd built a new one. In any case, she was a new girl in a new school. An outsider. That must have been before she met Caroline, she thinks. Perhaps she'll ask later. She remembers recess and lunch hours. She couldn't go home for lunch, not any more. The school was too far from her house, and so she stayed to eat her lunch and play. That was what you were expected to do in grade 3; at recess and at lunch you played with all the other little girls.

For a while, though, she couldn't. She was new. She stood at the edge of the cement slab that was painted with four-square and hop-scotch markings as if she were on her way from somewhere to some-where else. Suddenly the group of girls would pick up, a flock of starlings, and swoop off en masse, leaving her standing, wistful, pro-tective. Another girl wasn't part of the flock either, and they would stand together, watching the others at recess and at lunch and at recess. The other girl's name was Patty and she had two older sisters and a brother. 'And I've got a cat named Emily and she's going to have kittens. You can come see her, if you want.'

But then the flock descended and somehow she was a part of it. And she knew that Patty was a Jonnson and so had Jonnson fleas, just like her sisters and brother, and you could get them from her. Patty also, a solemn little girl advised Roberta, pees herself. And it was true. You could smell it. So those were Jonnson fleas.

Only there was more to it than that. Later, perhaps much later, Roberta overheard her favourite teacher in conversation. Telling another teacher that Patty Jonnson is in her class this year, and that she lies and perhaps steals. Like all the Jonnsons. And then the other teacher used a word, and they both laughed. And then her teacher saw Roberta standing there, and smiled at her. This is my favourite pupil, she said, and brushed Roberta's hair with her hand. So it must have been true.

The men have returned. They're still going on about computers. Roberta suspects that neither really knows what he is talking about, but that's part of the ritual as well. William, who has never as far as she knows been near a computer, is lecturing Peter on his choice of laptop. Men don't really have conversations, she thinks, they have serial monologues. Coffees are replenished and William and Peter join them in a liqueur. Their conversation smoothly segues to single malt scotch. Roberta knows that Caroline sees her observing the two men and must know what she's thinking. Caroline smiles at Roberta, sisters.

The origins of their friendship are lost to Roberta. They must have come after Jonnson fleas, Roberta thinks; she doesn't remember Caroline there. Had she been, or does she have her own version of the betrayal? Another question she can't ask. Later, of course, they became more subtle, approaching the knife-edge of adulthood. Later, position was won or lost with a glance, a gesture. Fleas, like all childish things, were the first awkward jerkings of what would become the social dance. God, listen to me, Roberta thinks, and smiles and nods at something Caroline has just said. What's got me in this mood?

But Caroline is thinking about their childhood as well. 'Do you remember when we met, Berta?' she asks, slipping comfortably back to the nickname Roberta no longer uses. 'In grade 4? And then you came to my birthday party, I think, and after that we were friends.'

Yes, Roberta remembers, that's so. She's able to recall a dim memory of the party, with Caroline the queen at the centre of a crowd of girls. Except, by the end of the afternoon it was Roberta who was at the centre, entertaining, organizing, it was Roberta who was the focus of the group. And it was Caroline who allowed it to happen, smiling, happy that her new friend was getting along so well. Which was, no doubt, the basis of their very long friendship and the root of Roberta's dislike: Caroline let you do those things to her. And that acceptance not only allowed such feelings, it practically demanded them. Caroline, standing at the side of the room, watching as her party, her friends, reformed about Roberta. Caroline smiling.

And again, now, Roberta can't stop herself from her feelings of

· · · 59 · · ·

love, her feelings of contempt. She realizes that, later on in the car driving home, she will try and she will fail to refrain from making snide comments to William about Caroline.

And Roberta thinks all these things, and wonders if Caroline does too. She must have some understanding of what Roberta thinks, who Roberta is. She must, for when they leave, there is an instant when she looks into Roberta's eyes. And in that instant, when they look at one another, Roberta is sure that neither of them knows what will be gained or what lost when they touch. They are suddenly nine years old, and forty-five, and all the ages they've been in between, and the rules of all games are not just more complicated, they are unsaid, unknown. And then they embrace, old friends, and the evening is over.

Black and White

LAJOS REACHES FOR HIS queen's bishop and then pauses, his hand hovering just above the piece. He withdraws the hand, taps at his teeth with his thumbnail, and squints down at the board. The hand moves back to its place over the bishop. Lajos can read far enough ahead to realize that something is happening, but not far enough to know what that something is. I say nothing.

If you win, you win in one of two ways. Some make their final move, throw 'checkmate' in their opponent's face, laugh. Some say nothing, show nothing, simply sit and watch as the other player discovers just exactly what has happened. Some win the first way, others the second. So, it's OK to laugh at the loss of another and it's OK to show nothing at all, but what you must never do is look pleased with yourself. Because this implies that there might have been some doubt, some question of the other prevailing. And that, for this group hunched over chessboards, these men that I call my friends, will never do.

Lajos, like me, is Hungarian. *Was* Hungarian, said properly, as we are all Canadians now. But we think of ourselves, still, as Hungarians, just as some of the others think of themselves as Czechs, Poles, even a couple of Russians. We've all come to Canada, most of us long ago, but we remain what we were. And one of the things we were, the only thing we have in common, the only thing that matters, is players of chess.

Lajos is in agony. His hand moves again for the bishop, but he knows now that this is not the move. The others crowded around our table argue amongst themselves, debating his play. 'What is his best move?' one of them says, answering another's question. 'His best move is to not play Gabor!' They laugh at this, but I do not. It is as if I haven't heard them. They are right, though, Lajos's first mistake was playing me.

He moves the bishop, as I knew he would. I do not respond right away, though I know my move. Instead I study the board, purse my lips, the image of a man lost in thought. A small gift that Lajos will never know he has received.

The centre closes at nine o'clock and I walk home. On the way I stop to buy a carton of milk, some bread, and on impulse a bunch of slightly sickly flowers. I have been married twenty-three years and in that time I've learned that it is the smallest of things that counts the most.

'How was the game?' my wife asks as she arranges the flowers in a vase, pleased. 'Did you win?'

I shrug. 'I did OK,' I say. 'Not too bad.'

She nods. 'You won.' There, now that the flowers are perfect we can sit, drink our cup of tea and watch the news.

My wife's name is Shelly, short for Michelle, though she has never used that name. She is a Canadian, I met her after I too had become a Canadian. Though I've been told that my English is now without accent and I believe this, she claims that I call her 'Zjelly'. Sometimes, if she is leaving me a note, she signs her name this way. Gabor and Zjelly. And now, after twenty-three years and even though 'sh' is not a sound a Hungarian has trouble with saying, maybe I do call her that because I know it pleases her.

After the news we go to bed. We read for a few minutes, maybe fifteen, Shelly from a stack of novels that lies on the floor next to her, while I flip through a chess journal, trying to think, if only for a move or two, like a grandmaster. Now it is I who tap at my teeth with a thumbnail, lost. Worse than lost, lost but almost not lost.

We each reach out, at the same time, for our reading lamps. We kiss good night, and lie in one another's arms for a few moments as we drift toward sleep. We have a good life, Shelly and I. I could trade it for no other.

I work all day, it's not important – not bad, just not important. Shelly and I have dinner, which we both prepare. We sit after dinner and read, or watch the television, and at seven o'clock I go out.

The others are there before me, with three tables set up. Rather, there is one long folding table with three plastic mats rolled out – each the regulation green and white squares of a chessboard. So, six

• • •   62   • • •

men sit at this table, playing, concentrating, while others cluster around insulting their play, laughing at their mistakes.

Even though others are waiting to play I am seated as soon as a game ends. It is a courtesy but also a right. It is immodest of me to say so, but I am the strongest player here and as such deserving of certain considerations. I could never demand them, of course, just as the others would never admit just why it is that I am seated first.

I play several games of blitz chess, winning each one. I enjoy blitz, it is more of a challenge to me, a breathless rush to complete all of a game's moves in under five minutes. In this game the real opponent is the clock, and we slap at it as we finish our moves, stopping our time and starting our opponent's. Move, slap, move, slap; it is exhilarating and exhausting, both. Chess becomes an almost physical act, and when the game is done I have the feeling of having bested my opponent not with my mind but with my greater strength and physical courage.

Then the strongest player, the strongest after me, that is, decides he will have a game. We reset the clocks and play a regulation game. He is good, this one, and getting better; I will have to watch out for him. I don't know his name. I've played chess against him for maybe ten years and a day comes when you can no longer ask. I don't know if anyone here knows his name, but everyone knows he is the best player in this room, after me. He wears, always, a chequered cap and I think of him as Kalap, which is the Hungarian word for hat.

I win this game too. I almost always win and when I lose I realize it before my opponent. A small mistake, an oversight, an insignificant move made in haste and a game begins to slip away. This is the beauty of chess, this struggle for perfection; and, always, the game recedes in front of us. No matter how much I study, no matter how many games I play, there is more to be learned, many more games to be won and occasionally lost.

A young guy is hanging around. He's maybe thirty, perhaps a bit older, tall and thin, and an intense student of our games. He is the only outsider, which is why I notice him. Everyone else belongs, a longtime player, but I have not seen this man before. He stands back, just a little, as if he knows this is not yet his place. He watches our board intently, now nodding his head in agreement, now shaking it ever so slightly when he disagrees. My opponent makes a very bad move, though he will not know it for three or four more moves, and I hear the Young Guy speak. 'No,' he says, under his breath, as if the word escaped from his control. So I know that he is a player and I know that he is a good one.

But I don't play him. I don't even talk to him, no one does. This is not some club you can join, drop in for a casual game once in a while. If he wants a place here, he must earn it. Lajos notices him too. *Who's the split-ass?* he says to me in Hungarian. 'Senki,' I say. Nobody, nobody at all. Lajos and I laugh and the Young Guy chuckles to himself, trying to fit in, thinking that we're talking about the game I am about to win. I feel a quick shiver of shame at this. In Hungarian we have a saying: to grow a second face. I feel a bit that I have done this, but there is nothing I can do.

He stays there, watching, the whole night until the centre closes and we all must leave, and he plays not a single game.

He keeps coming back. He says nothing, never asks to play, just stands there watching the games. After a week of this he's not exactly welcome, but he's no longer unwelcome. We have become used to seeing him standing there, nodding his head at what he sees happening on the three green-and-white boards.

When he finally gets a game it is not with me, of course. I'm playing two boards at once, winning against two mediocre players. For some reason the crowd is thin tonight, so it's OK that I take up two spaces. The third board is, in fact, empty. Kalap sits back, arms crossed, staring down at the pieces lined up in their ranks, waiting for someone to challenge him. A few people stand around, but they are only tourists, watchers; they count for nothing. The only player, standing a little way back watching me play, watching Kalap wait, is the Young Guy.

Kalap grunts and nods his head at the board. The Young Guy nods back and sits down.

I pay attention to my own games for a while. I amuse myself by attempting odd combinations and patterns; I tell myself that to win on one board I cannot use my queen or one of my rooks. On the other board I must promote a pawn to win, even though this is quite unnecessary. With the two wood pushers I am facing, I am forced to amuse myself. There will be nothing to see on the board beside me for several moves, anyway. Even a monkey can memorize a few opening patterns, learn the first dozen moves of a brilliant game. After that, well, what comes after means everything.

I help one of the wood pushers out, small hints, suggestions. He's trying to improve and he has respect, so why not? I try to help him make the best of his game; we work together to make the most beautiful game possible. So I can take amusement even from a game against a weak player.

The other one though, he has a bad attitude. I've played him before and it was just the same: when he loses it is because of bad luck, and he resigns with ill grace. When he wins, not against me, but when he wins it is all he can do to refrain from doing a little dance. This man is a worshipper of Luck and Pride. He will never be a chess player. I do not say one word to him and I will defeat him the way I would slap a mosquito.

I've forgotten about Kalap and the Young Guy. When I look at their board I see that they are well into the mid-game. Both white and black look solid; neither is taking any chances and neither has committed any errors. Patterns are emerging on both sides but they are subtle, there but almost not there. With weak players the line of play is laid out like a mouth across a face, an expression that anyone may read. I'd expected Kalap to play an artistic game, but the Young Guy is a surprise. I think that maybe this one can really play.

I toy with my own games for a while and when I next look over it is because Kalap swears softly under his breath. He takes off his cap and rakes his hair with his fingers. He mutters again, searching for an escape, but there is none. He is forced to make a desperate move and I see that this game will go to the Young Guy. Kalap's one chance is if his opponent makes a facile move, takes an easy check and allows Kalap to slip away. I watch, my own games ignored for this moment, and the Young Guy makes the expert move. Kalap is doomed. I turn back to my games.

When I first came over, after the uprising in '56, I spoke almost no English. I had no skills, either, I was no electrician or bricklayer, someone who could work no matter what his language. I had intended to be a scholar. When I was fourteen years old I had decided that I would become a professor of mathematics. That was also the time when I first began to seriously study chess. So, I did not lose everything when I left Hungary. And I've learned that the things that matter most are the ones you can carry within you. These things can never be taken away.

I learned the language. I got a job, with a company that operates oceangoing tugboats. I worked in the boat-yard, sweeping up. Then, but only for a short time, I was a swamper on one of the smaller tugs. And then, and then. I still work for the same company; I've been there long enough that I have an office, I have a neat little box of business cards that I don't use.

I met Shelly and got married. We have a little apartment and, for reasons that are unclear, no children. I play chess every night and Shelly understands. Life isn't so bad.

I am not surprised, when I arrive the next night, to see the Young Guy seated behind a board. Of course he has won his games, I had expected that. The seat across from him is empty and I had expected that too. It is time for us to play.

I remove my coat and scarf, hang them on the coat-rack, and sit down. The Young Guy nods and smiles slightly and I nod back. He has given me white, which is the courteous thing, and I open with my king's pawn. He responds with his own king's pawn and I continue with the standard opening. After his third move, however, his bishop to king two, he looks up at me and smiles as if he expects something. It takes a second before I realize what he has done. There is a name for his move; he has played the Hungarian Defence. My ears burn. What does he mean by this? How am I supposed to take this move of his? I smile for him, what else can I do, then push a man forward. Concentrate, I tell myself. Concentrate, Gabor.

'You're home early,' Shelly says, 'how did it go?'
    'Fine,' I say. 'We broke up early. The games were fine.'

In bed I lie with my eyes open, replaying the game in my head, trying to see just when it went wrong. It was close, and a difficult game for both of us, but at some point, some point that I am now trying to isolate, I began to lose. And, worst of all, I was aware at the time what was happening. Everybody loses, everybody makes mistakes; but to see a game slowly slipping away from you, water between your fingers, so that no matter how hard you try to hold on, well.... The next was just the same, and the next. Damn.

At dinner the next day I eat with a chess book open on the table next to me.

'Gabor,' Shelly says.

I look up, laying my hand on the pages so my place will not be lost.

'Gabor, what's going on?'

I shrug. 'Nothing,' I say. 'I was just curious about something. Nothing.'

Shelly nods and goes back to her meal. She knows I am lying but it is not our way to talk about these things. What could I say to her?

I leave immediately after dinner. I want to get there first; I want to be the one who holds the table when the Young Guy arrives. A small thing, but still I hurry along the street. A foolish man, rushing off to reclaim a trifle.

There is a good crowd there already. Maybe they've heard, maybe not. I do my best not to notice. Lajos finishes a game and I sit down. Lajos is always there early and I think, truthfully, that he has not much else in his life.

We have a good game, a difficult game. When I win it feels good, not so much because of the win but because of the struggle. I know that I can face an excellent player like Lajos and prevail.

Next the wood pusher from the other night, the one with a poor attitude, wants to play. I dislike this man and maybe I don't behave as well as I might. With him I play a brutal game, a humiliating game, and soon he is gone. Lajos, who has been watching, laughs at the way I have treated him, and I smile in return. *Thank you, come again,* says Lajos.

A small muttering runs through the six or seven men who are crowded in our corner, and a few look toward the entrance. The glass door swings opens and the Young Guy walks in.

'Gabor, what is it?' Shelly will not leave me alone. 'What is bothering you?'

'Nothing is wrong!' I bellow. Then, lowering my voice, 'I'm sorry Shelly, maybe I'm a little out of sorts. I'm not feeling well, the flu, I think.' I avoid her eye and, tossing my coat and scarf on the sofa, go into the bathroom.

With the door closed and locked I lean on the counter, staring down at the patterns in the false marble. To lose is one thing; to make an error, a lapse in concentration – there are always other games, other players. But to not see, to be unable to know how or why one has failed. It is a terrible thing. It is a thing that cannot be happening to me.

The next night, as we're finishing the dishes, I say in what I hope is an offhand way, 'Why don't we spend the evening together, maybe go for a walk.' I hand a plate to Shelly, the last one, and she rubs it dry.

'That would be nice, Gabor,' she says, 'that sounds like it would be very nice.' She is watching me and I turn away to wipe the counter, drain the sink of its soapy water. She pats me on the shoulder, gives me a small hug, but doesn't say anything more. How did she come to know me so well, this woman, what have I done to deserve someone as good as her?

We walk the few blocks to the shoreline and then along the seawall. The seawall is crowded but not unpleasantly so. People walking in pairs, slowly riding bicycles, shuddering along on those new roller-skates that are suddenly everywhere. Shelly and I hold hands as we walk, neither of us speaking, headed towards Stanley Park.

'It's a beautiful evening,' Shelly says. And it is, warm but with a touch of cold creeping in, just the kind of weather I like. The sun will be going down soon, and the sunset will be spectacular.

'Yes,' I say. 'We should do this every night. How would you like to do this every night?'

Shelly stops walking and looks at me, her face concerned. 'Gabor,' she says, 'what is it?'

I start walking again. 'Nothing,' I say. 'I'd forgotten how beautiful this all is,' I say.

But when we're lying in bed a thought strikes me. My mistake has been that I've always believed that there is just one kind of game, one perfect game lying undiscovered there in the jumble of the board, waiting to be revealed. But of course that is not true. I sit up, excited, amazed at my stupidity. If your opponent plays a forceful game, you must never meet that force head on. This is obvious, this is something every player of chess should know. You must counter strength with cunning, cunning with strength. The Young Guy prevailed because I was foolish enough to play his game for him. But now I am wise enough to know what a fool I'd been. And tomorrow he will see that Gabor can play many different flavours of chess. I chuckle to myself, I practically rub my hands together I am so pleased. Something makes me look over at Shelly, looking back at me, smiling.

'So, Gabor,' Shelly says, 'No walk tomorrow?'

But he beats me again. It is impossible, but it happens. When I arrive, the Young Guy is waiting for me. The others, all the others, are waiting as well, watching. And what they get to see is not much. One, two, three, the Young Guy tears me apart. I thank him for the games, retrieve my hat and coat, and then I walk away. The door swings shut behind me, I button my coat against the cool of the night, and I think: I can never go back; this has ended for me now.

'Gabor,' Shelly says to me, it's been two days and I haven't been to play chess, I've packed all my books and journals back on the bookshelves, 'Gabor.' I am sitting on the edge of the ottoman, fooling with the TV, looking for something, anything in its sea of inanity. Shelly sighs, but I stay hunched over, fiddling with the little buttons, perusing one second, two, of each station before it is on to the next.

I hear the door open and I turn around. Shelly stands in the open doorway, my hat and coat in her hands. 'Go, Gabor,' she says. 'Just go.'

Hey, Gabor, long time no see, Lajos says to me in Hungarian, but softly, almost a whisper. As if even in this language that we share he does not want to embarrass me in front of the others.

A day, a lifetime, an afternoon, I say, the punch line to an old joke from the old country, and we both chuckle. I shrug off my coat and take the chance to look around. Kalap is here, he already holds a board and is playing against a middleweight player. Some of the others, wood pushers mostly, all familiar faces. Kalap's is the only board in use. The Young Guy is not yet here.

Come on, Lajos says, *I need the aggravation*, and sits down at the board. And we have a good game. I give Lajos a couple of pointers, but not too much. I'm careful to make sure it's OK with him, that my instruction is not seen as an insult. But it's OK, Lajos doesn't seem to mind. In fact he seems to appreciate it, though nothing much is said.

After I've beaten him we play through a few of the decisive moves, trying to see what other opportunities Lajos had. He nods his head as I offer a counter, play through a few moves, then reset the position. 'OK,' Lajos says. He's smiling now, able to see the pattern. 'Ertem, értem,' he says. *Yes, I see, I see.*

'Hey, Gabor,' someone says. I look up and see that everyone is looking at me. Kalap, even the wood pusher with the bad attitude, everyone, all looking at me, smiling, nodding. 'Good to see you back,' someone says, but that is going too far and now the others return to their games, to their arguments, whatever. Still.

Lajos resets the board and opens with his king's pawn. I reply, but then Lajos's eyes flick to the front doors. Something crosses his face and I don't have to turn in my seat to know who has just entered. 'Your move,' I say.

Right, right, Lajos mutters, sliding his queen's pawn. I reply and he replies and so the game goes. I win, but not so easily. Lajos, despite the fact that he plays each night, I have never considered a serious player. Now, who knows? Maybe my mistake was that I considered myself a serious player.

We reset the board and Lajos rises from his chair, making space for the next player. It is the Young Guy who has been waiting, as I knew he would. And, though I came here hoping that everything would go my way, now I know that it cannot. As rain falls from the sky, so the Young Guy will best me in this thing to which I have devoted so much of myself.

But before he can sit down, Kalap moves over. 'No,' he says, 'I was waiting. My turn to play Gabor.'

What can the Young Guy do? He smiles, shrugs, and steps back to let Kalap sit down. Kalap doesn't even look at me, just frowns at the board and then begins with a knight's opening.

We both play slowly, more slowly than usual. And we play a good game, together we create a game that is really something. When I win I am disappointed that it is over. Kalap nods, once, twice, then pushes back his chair. I rise too and hold out my hand, thanking him for his game.

Now the Young Guy moves forward again, to claim what is his. But someone else taps him on the shoulder, another of the regular players whose name is, I think, Peter. 'No, you are mistaken,' he says. 'I am next to play Gabor.'

And after Peter it is Hermann. And then someone whose name I have forgotten. And then, impossibly, Lajos pushes forward again. 'You will excuse me, I think,' he says to the Young Guy. 'It has been so long since I have played with my friend Gabor, here.' And now I see that this is not one large group but one group and one man and that one man is no longer welcome. The Young Guy sees it too, but for a moment he just stands there, doing nothing, saying nothing. Then, still without expression or sound, he walks away, across the floor and out the swinging front doors. Lajos sits.

But I do not respond to his move. I stare after the Young Guy, though he is gone from view. I stand. 'No,' I say. 'My friends, no. This is not right.'

I push my way out from behind the table and hurry across the floor. I push through the door and step out into the half-light of the evening. Though I stand in the middle of the sidewalk and look first in one direction and then the opposite, I cannot see him. I walk the half block to the corner and look to see if he has gone down the side street, but there is no one there. 'Damn!' I mutter to myself. 'Damn, damn, damn!'

When I re-enter the community centre they are all looking at me. They've saved my place; the board is as it was, one pawn pushed forward awaiting my response. And as they smile and help me to my place I know for the first time that these men are my true friends and that together we have done a terrible thing.

Limited Time Offer

THE PHONE RANG. I was in the middle of eating my dinner, such as it was, and turned to look at the phone hanging there on the wall. The cat stopped eating his dinner and looked at me. He can ignore phone calls, something I'm still learning to do. It's never more than a wrong number or, usually, someone who hasn't heard about Nadine and me. They ask about Nadine and then I have to go into the whole song and dance – better to let it ring. The cat's got the right idea. Now that it's just the two of us, I let him eat on the table. He's got his own place mat, which he sits on, and then it's me and him, the two guys at dinner.

But the phone kept ringing. Finally I got up to answer it. What the hell.

'Is this Mr Willis Gallat?' the voice asked. A woman's voice, trying to sound excited and pleasant. Pleasant and excited.

'Who's this?' I said.

She told me her name was Blanche, which made me pay attention, because you don't hear that name very often. And then she took a breath, I heard a rustling of paper, and she went for it. Real estate. Zero down financing. Master of your own independence. Limited time, special once-only reduced introductory lecture. Like that. Yadda, yadda, yadda. Every third sentence she threw in my name, to remind me that we were friends. Mr Gallat this, Mr Gallat that. By the end of the spiel, where she was telling me about the seminar she wanted me to attend – no obligation, coffee and cake, free gifts – she was calling me Willis.

'Now, does this sound like something you can afford to pass up, Willis? You tell me. Does this Thursday sound like something you can afford to pass up?'

I tried to imagine this woman on the end of the phone. Who was she, what did she look like? I didn't have much luck. 'Today's Tuesday,' I said, like that meant something. Then, when she didn't reply: 'Tell me, Blanche,' I said. 'Are you going to be there?'

She made a little noise at the end of the phone, I'm not sure what. 'I'll be there, Willis,' she said.

The day Nadine left, she shook my hand. Married twenty-nine years and it all ends with a handshake. I stood in the doorway and watched as she backed her car down the drive. She stopped at the end, looked both ways, then pulled into the street. Everything was just a little bit slower than normal, as if we were both being careful, watching what we did. Just as she pulled away she beeped the horn and I waved.

After I got off the phone and had a chance to think about it, I tried on a couple of different ties and thought they looked pretty good. The thing is, you can never tell if they're still in fashion. I thought about it some more and decided that I didn't want to look over-dressed, so maybe open collar. I pulled out my Harris tweed sport jacket. The lining is shot but you wouldn't notice, and it hangs well. Knowing what I would wear took a little bit of the edge off. I hung the coat and the rest of it back up, all set. How many guys, right now, were getting themselves all dolled up for Blanche, I wondered. I shook my head at myself and went back to my cold spaghetti.

When I got home from work the next day, Nadine's car was in the driveway. She drops by once or twice a week, to pick up her mail and whatnot. It's like having a visit from a cousin you've never met: you know that they're family, but you can no longer quite remember how or why. A little bit more than a stranger, a little bit less than something else.

She was sitting on one end of the sofa with the cat, the traitor, asleep in her lap. 'Hello, Willis,' she said.

'Hello, Nadine.' I went and hung up my coat. Then, child that I am, I opened the fridge door, something that usually brings the cat running. I closed it again and went back into the living room. He hadn't budged. 'Can I get you something?' I asked.

'Tea?'

I nodded. 'Tea. Right.' I went back into the kitchen to boil the water. And, each in our own room, things felt a little easier. Nadine called after me.

'Everything OK, Willis? Are you doing all right, here?'

I filled the kettle and plugged it in. I looked around for something I could serve with it. 'Yes,' I said, raising my voice just a little, just enough so that it would sound normal in the other room, 'I'm getting along pretty well.' I found a box of biscuits, really nothing more than fancy crackers, and dumped some into a bowl. Tea at Tiffany's. 'How about you?'

There was a pause from the other room, then: 'Oh, you know. Fine.' I picked out two tea mugs and set them on a tray, along with the biscuits. I didn't bother with cream or sugar since Nadine and I both drink it clear. The water was boiling and I fixed the tea.

When I carried the stuff into the other room I was surprised to see that Nadine was standing up. She was over by the mantelpiece, casually inspecting this and that. The way guests do, killing time. I put the tea down on the coffee table and pulled up a chair.

Nadine sat on the couch. I poured her tea for her, then my own. We sat there, holding our mugs.

'So,' she said. 'I'm glad that everything is O K.'

I nodded. 'Everything is fine. Just fine.' I blew on my tea.

'And you're getting out? You're meeting people, getting out of the house?'

'Sure, sure,' I said. 'You don't have to worry about me, Nadine.'

She sipped her tea and thought about that, about whether she had to worry about me or not. 'I know it's been hard, Willis, and I know that you. . . .' She tapered off, her words disappearing into the air, then sipped at her tea some more.

'As a matter of fact,' I said, 'I'm seeing someone. I've been seeing someone for a little while.'

She smiled for me, a genuine smile if a little brittle around the edges. 'Really? That's wonderful, that's really wonderful, Willis. Do I know her?'

I shook my head. 'Her name is Blanche. Isn't that something? Blanche.' I petted the cat, running my hand back and forth, up and down his spine. 'We're seeing one another. You know.'

Nadine was still smiling. 'Willis, that's fine. I'm so glad.'

'Me, too,' I said. 'Me, too.' I scratched the cat's ears, turning one inside out then letting it flop back. 'It's nothing serious,' I said. 'You know.'

'Sure,' she said. 'Sure.'

The cat hopped down and wandered off, ignoring both of us.

The seminar was at seven-thirty, so I had time for a shower. I shaved again too, what the hell. It's nice to have the luxury of time – a long shower, fresh blade in the razor, no frantic rushing off like in the morning.

After I patted my face dry I stood there, checking myself out in the mirror. I turned sideways, then face front again, then turned to the other side. I don't know. Maybe we all fool ourselves, but I don't think I looked that bad. I slapped my gut, hard, and tried to stand a little straighter.

Back in the bedroom I thought about what kind of a lover I'd been to Nadine. You can make yourself crazy with this, Willis, I told myself, but I didn't stop. I think probably everyone wonders. And, on balance I was probably pretty good. Not like in the movies, of course, but who is? I wonder if anyone can measure up to all of that sort of thing. I wonder what it's like to be an actor and have to compete with yourself when you get home at night. Must be a hell of a thing. I finished drying myself and got dressed.

The seminar was in a community centre I'd never heard of that turned out to be less than twenty blocks from my house. I pulled into the parking lot at quarter after seven and had to drive around twice to find a space. I sat, drumming my fingers on the steering wheel, and wondered just what the hell I was doing. You're going to a real estate seminar, Willis, that's what you're doing. I might even have said this out loud, but there was no one to hear. All those cars and not a soul in sight. Maybe the seminar would be full and I could leave right away. I'd give it ten minutes and then I'd leave, that would be more than fair.

I got out of the car and I had to force myself not to check my hair in the rear view mirror before I did so. The hell with it. Ten minutes.

Just inside the door was a cluster of upholstered chairs and low tables. A small group of men stood hunched around one of the tables, watching two men play chess. I moved over to watch too, not quite joining the group but watching all the same. The players seemed good, at least they moved very quickly, and they slapped at one of those double clocks after every move. I don't know much about chess, so I couldn't have said much even if I was inclined to, but the crowd of men watching, six or seven, would murmur, laugh, insult whoever had just moved. They all had some kind of eastern European accent. Maybe they were Russians, who knows? Maybe they were exiled grandmasters.

Someone had positioned an easel with one of those white plastic boards you write on with coloured felt pens. 'Success Seminar,' it said, and told me to go to room 205. It had a red arrow, pointing up. All the S's were in green, and crossed like dollar signs. I shook my head and looked for the stairs. I wondered what the chess guys thought about all this, if they thought about it at all.

More signboards showed the way to room 205. People were clumped in twos and threes all down the hall and from the sound coming out of 205 it was pretty packed in there. I had to check in at a little card table they had set up just in front of the door, tell them my name and paste a name-tag, Willis Gillette, close enough, to my lapel. I'd hoped that Blanche would be there, right out front where I could see her, but it was someone named Kathy Kousins with two K's. She used a green felt pen to print my name and her smile was as bright as a bug-light. No good will come of this, Willis, I told myself, and walked in.

The room was packed with people. Most of them looked like they'd spent some time wondering whether to wear a tie or not. Lots of sports jackets that hadn't been aired recently, lots of people milling around trying to look relaxed and rattlesnake-sharp at the same time. Every now and again you'd catch sight of someone in a full suit, expensive suit, and you'd know he was with the outfit. Their name-tags were plastic, professionally printed. OK, I thought, you've made a mistake there, you've pointed out that we're different, that you're not one of us. Figuring this out made me feel better, like I had something on them. I looked around, trying to guess what Blanche would look like.

I couldn't see her. From her voice on the phone, the way she talked, and from her name, Blanche, not one you hear much any more, I had her figured to be a certain age. I'd guess fifty, which would be nice, two years younger than me. I looked around for a pleasant-looking woman of about fifty. For some reason I assumed she'd be wearing a sweater.

The place was packed. And everyone was doing more or less what I was, which was fidgeting, glancing now and again at the stage that was set up with a lecture stand and various props – charts, more white boards, that sort of thing. No one was on the stage.

I was reminded of something but I couldn't put my finger on it. A whole stream of people came through the door, shooed in by one of the guys in the good suits, so I knew the show was starting. And then I remembered, the shooing business brought it back.

When Nadine and I were first married we joined a dance group. A group for people like us, couples, married people, who wanted to learn to ballroom dance. The thing that reminded me was that it was held in the gym of a school we lived near at the time. The suits reminded me too, everybody dolled up just a little more than they were comfortable with, but careful not to overdo it. We probably wore ties, though, things were a bit more formal then.

And it was exactly the same. A group of people waiting for something, half dreading it, and other people shooing them here and there, organizing. Just the same.

I think Nadine had actually liked it quite a bit, she was more of a dancer than me, more of a socializer, too. I don't need that many people in my life. I'm not comfortable with crowds of people around me, even if they're friends. Even so, I probably should have stuck with the dancing. I told Nadine she could go by herself, if she liked it she should keep on going, but it wasn't for me. Now, I'd probably go with her. Not such a big thing.

The lights dimmed and we all turned to look at the stage. One of the sharpies who'd been working the audience jumped onto it and jogged over to the lecture stand. Nothing but energy, this guy, nothing but get-up-and-go.

He clipped a tiny wireless microphone to his lapel and then walked forward so he was standing right at the edge of the stage. He looked out at us, taking his time, really playing it up. He unbuttoned his jacket and put his hands on his hips, still studying us, like he was personally checking on each one of us. And I knew we were in for a show, all right. I knew that in about two minutes flat this sharpie would have us snapping like mackerel at whatever he threw at us.

And he did. Boy, did he ever. He started by leaning out, so far over the edge I thought he just might keep on going, but of course he didn't. 'Are you ready?' he cried, his voice booming through the speakers like God's older brother. 'Are you ready to take control of your own life?'

He finished, after an hour of the biggest razzle-dazzle I'd ever seen – now on the stage, now walking through the audience, asking questions and then answering them for himself, slapping people on the back, running, skipping, telling jokes, recounting sad tales of warning – he finished, back on the stage, back where he started, leaning out over us, his voice low, sincere, the voice of the best friend we had in the world. 'It's your life,' he whispered, 'it's in your hands.'

And that was the show. Boy, was that the show. Of course it was just starting. He had us all frothed up, rapturous. We were *his*. And now it was time to reel us in. He could have told us to squat on the floor and bark like seals and we would have done it. It was something, to be caught up in all that, it was really something.

The next thing you knew everyone was crowded around one or another of the sharpies – who had clipboards now and were writing away as if their lives depended on it. They didn't have to work the crowd any more; the crowd was working *them*. People were frantic to get at them, like this opportunity we'd spent the last hour hearing about might just disappear, *poof*, and then where would we be?

But I hung back. I had been as caught up as the next guy, I'll admit that, but now the lights were back on and my head was beginning to clear. Nadine says I'm suspicious by nature and maybe that's so. It's kept me out of a lot of trouble.

And I wasn't the only one. Maybe half the crowd was still milling around. Not leaving the room, mind, but not rushing right over, either. Waiting to be seduced or scared off, one or the other.

They'd thought of that, too. Now that I was watching I noticed a number of women and men trolling through the crowd. These weren't the sharpies, these were something else. They'd stop and ask a question of whoever, then chat for a few seconds, a minute. They were all touchers, they all touched the arm of the person they were talking with, likely something they'd been trained to do. And then they were walking together, still talking, still arm-touching, over to one of the sharpies. And this sharpie would make a big deal, a *big* deal about the whole thing. This wasn't just anybody they were being introduced to, this was.... And that was another one, bought, sold, delivered. It was truly something to see.

A woman was standing in front of me, smiling at me. She was my age and her hair looked freshly done, but like she'd done it herself. A nice look, a nice-looking woman.

'Willis,' she said, 'I'm so glad you could come.'

I must have stared at her, because she laughed. She tapped her lapel and the name-tag there. 'I'm Blanche,' she said. 'Do you remember we talked on the phone?'

Blanche. I thought of all the things that had gone through my mind, of trying on different ties, of saying ridiculous things to Nadine. And I knew that in a second Blanche would put her hand on my arm and I would be magically, effortlessly guided over to one of the sharpies with his clipboard and his pen. I don't even have a name for the way I felt right then.

'Willis? Is something wrong?' Blanche was staring at me, concerned. Looking concerned, anyhow.

I shook my head. 'No. Nothing's wrong. I have to go, though. I can't stay here.' I half expected her to put her hand on me then, that would have been the time. A gentle touch to show concern, and then maybe I'd like to talk about it with one of the sharpies....

But she didn't. She stood there, looking up at me, thinking about something. She stood there for a long time, a lot longer than you would expect someone to look at you, not saying anything. 'It's all this, isn't it?' She turned and looked at the room, thinning now of people as they were all processed and then hustled out the door. 'This is what's bothering you.' She turned back to me, nodding her head. 'I took this job for the money, of course, but also because I like people. That was the main thing, it was a chance to meet people, but now I don't know.' She looked around again, as if things would suddenly come clear. 'I'm beginning to wonder about these people, Willis, I really am. They just seem a little smooth to me. A little smooth.' Again she stopped but kept looking at me, directly in my eyes. 'I don't know if I can recommend them to you. I'm sorry that I got you involved with them.'

She held out her hand. 'It was nice to meet you, Willis.'

Now it was my turn to stare. I wasn't exactly sure what was going on, but I knew that I was only the smallest part of it. I took her hand and we shook. Then Blanche did a funny thing. She reached and pulled my sticky name-tag from my suit. Then she pulled hers off – it was just a sticky one, too, not the kind the sharpies wore – and crumpled them up. She held the wad of sticky paper in her hand for a second, like she didn't know what to do with it, then she handed it to me. 'Goodbye, Willis,' she said.

I crammed the paper into my jacket pocket. 'Goodbye, Blanche.' I watched her walk across the room, gather up a coat and bag, and walk out. I was still standing there, wondering if I should go after her, what I should do, when I felt a hand on my shoulder. The sharpie didn't even get a chance to speak before I shrugged him off and charged from the room. But Blanche was gone.

A week or so went by. I hadn't seen Nadine for a while and then she dropped by, catching me eating a peanut butter sandwich for dinner. I showed her in and made a big to-do about making tea – I don't know where I picked that up, it's not something I ever did when she and I were together, but now you can't drop by my place without getting pot-loads of tea forced on you. It's a gesture of some kind, I suppose, though I'm not one to go too deeply into that kind of analysis.

Nadine had some mail for me that had been misdirected to her house. When we got that all straightened around, and Nadine settled on the couch with a mug of tea and the cat, we pretty much ran out of things to say. It's not something you think about, but you do most of your talking with people you don't know very well. Once you're better acquainted, intimate, you've pretty well said it. And when you're forced to become strangers again it's hard to drag all those words up. And then it's hard when you realize that you can't.

'So,' she said, 'how's Blanche?'

'Who?' I said, at just the same time I realized who she meant. I sipped at my tea and watched Nadine watching me. I shrugged my shoulders. 'She's fine,' I said, 'but I don't think it's going to work out. You know.'

When Nadine left I stood in the doorway for a while, watching her drive away. I stood there for quite a while, holding the door with one hand, looking down the street.

I had to sort through all the junk in my wallet twice before I found the card. They'd passed them out when we first got our name-tags and I'd put mine away. Now I held it in my hand: Success Inc., it said, along with a phone number embossed in gold. What the hell, I told myself. Still, it took me a while before I actually phoned the number.

No, the woman said, Blanche wasn't there, but could she interest me in an opportunity that was limited.... It took a lot of persistence, more than I usually show, before I could discover that Blanche didn't work there any more. No, they didn't know where I might reach her and they were forbidden to give out her full name. However, they did have something they were certain I would be interested in – I hung up, cutting the woman off in mid-sentence.

I was almost asleep, that night, when I opened my eyes and said out loud: 'The name-tags.' I got out of bed and went to the closet. I put my tweed jacket on over my pyjamas and then dug my hands into the pockets. And, yes, there was the sticky clump that Blanche had handed me.

It took me a long time, hunched over the dining-room table, to separate the sticky pieces of paper. I wound up ripping them, of course, so I was more doing a jig-saw puzzle than anything else. It probably took me an hour, sitting there in bare feet, pyjamas, and a tweed sport coat with its lining shot, before I got it. Blanche Osbourne. Her last name was Osbourne. I left the tag stuck to the wood of the table and went back to bed.

I left the tag stuck there for three days. I'd pick at it while I was eating my cereal, maybe cover it with a plate at dinnertime but still know it was there. I looked her name up in the phone book so many times that I found I'd memorized it. But I didn't phone.

I cleaned the house. I made an effort to start cooking real meals, no more peanut butter sandwiches. I figured, OK, you've wallowed in being a bachelor long enough, time to start living like a human being. I made the cat eat his dinner on the floor, something neither of us thought was quite fair, but there you go.

Finally, one night I sat down and I figured out how many days it had been. More than two weeks, and a line of some kind was fast approaching. If I left it any longer Blanche wouldn't remember who I was, if she even still did. If she ever really had. I picked up the phone.

I put the phone back down. She wouldn't remember me. Worse, she'd pretend that she did, not wanting to hurt my feelings. I stared at the phone, trapped, furious with myself.

I think Nadine has a boyfriend now. She doesn't tell me about it, probably because she figures, rightly, that I don't want to know. But I'm OK with it. Enough time has passed and all that. Plus, I truly want her to be happy. Saying it that way makes me sound like I'm giving her something, but I'm not. I'm passive in this; all I can hope to be is a bystander, watching this woman I once knew, still half know, and hope that everything works out for her.

Maybe once a week I wonder how it could have been different, what I could have done. And the answer is always the same, nothing. I'd have to be a different person, that's all. Nadine might even have said that, the day she left, I can't remember. She told me she didn't blame me. I remember that because she kept saying it. I don't blame you, Willis.

If I'd been another kind of man I would have drunk a bottle of whisky, or broken things, Nadine's things. Another man might have picked up a woman somewhere, wherever it is they do that. I went to bed after the news, slept soundly, and was early for work the next day. Maybe there's something lacking in me, I suspect that's what Nadine was missing in me, anyway, but I can't be any other way than the way I am. I don't think that any of us can.

When she answered I found myself speaking all in a rush, as if I had to get to a certain point in the conversation before she had a chance to hang up. I could hear myself though, how silly and desperate I sounded, and I stopped. I was staring hard at the dial of the phone, focusing entirely on the little circles that hold your fingers. Someone, maybe me, had run a pen around and around the 6, a little blue circle around only that one hole. MNO. I hadn't noticed that before.

'Of course I remember you, Willis. Of course I do,' she said, and I believed her, I believed that she wasn't just saying what anyone would say to be polite.

And then she told me that she was hoping I would call. She actually told me that. That she felt badly about that night and was wondering if she'd hear from me.

I asked her if she'd like to get a coffee sometime. A coffee and dessert, maybe, at one of those places. If she'd like.

She'd like just fine, she said. That would be just fine. And we made a date, though that's probably not the right word, but we agreed to meet the next night at a place Blanche knew.

I was still staring at the phone after I'd hung up, amazed with myself, at how easy it had been. And angry with myself for all the nonsense I'd put myself through. I probably sat there for five minutes, just sitting.

The phone rang. 'Hello, Willis,' Blanche said.

Oh, I thought, here it comes. This is what you get, Willis. This is what happens. I took a deep breath. 'Look, Blanche, maybe it would –'

'Willis. I wanted to tell you that you should have more confidence. You're an attractive man, an intelligent and attractive man. I believe that a person needs to hear that now and again. I'll see you tomorrow, Willis.' She hung up.

I sat listening to the dial tone for probably a minute, just listening, not wanting to hang up on what I'd heard. And when I did replace the phone in its cradle I still sat there. It's odd, but you want to hang back, hold back for just a moment or two. Because you want to keep that feeling for as long as you can, that feeling of movement. I was old enough and smart enough to know that maybe things would work out with me and Blanche and maybe not, but I also knew that, whatever happened, I was happy about it, happy to be moving on.

The cat jumped onto my lap. 'Now how about that?' I asked him. 'What do you think of all that?' He was hungry so I went and opened a whole can of tuna for him. What the hell, live a little.

Monsters

DEVON SLAPS THE WATER with his hands and laughs. He has discovered that if he hits the water just so, the waves will crash against Daddy's belly. Each time his palms smack the water he laughs – slap, laugh, slap, laugh – each moment fresh, a new delight. Here is a thing that can't help but amuse him. He giggles, caught up in something wonderful.

I flick a finger at him, catching the surface of the water and sending a thin arc that bounces off his chest. He stops for a second, amazed at this new thing that can be done with only water and hands, and then giggles. 'Daddeee,' he cries, and pushes his right hand at the water. He lacks the coordination to mimic what I've done, but not for long.

'Deeeeevon,' I moo back at him. I take the facecloth from the side of the tub and rub it with soap. Devon is still trying to master the water flick while I scrub his chest. He sits still when it's time for his face, though, closing his eyes with a grimace, snorting through his nose. I run the soapy cloth around his neck, poke a finger into his ears, scrub my little boy clean. When I'm done he leans forward, eyes still firmly shut, and I cup water in my hands and splash his face to rinse it.

'There,' I say. 'All done.' But Devon still sits with his eyes closed, face scrunched up, a two-year-old old man. I lean close, till my nose almost touches his. 'Devon?' I say. 'Are you all right? Did Daddy get soap in your eyes?'

His eyes fly open. 'Boo!' he says, and I hug him, shaking him from side to side, setting up a series of waves that can't help but crash over the side. A very reasonable price to pay.

The phone rings while we're towelling dry. I hear Gillie answer it, the murmur of her voice if not the words. I can tell from the rhythms that the call isn't for her, but I keep drying Devon. Whoever is on the phone, I'll call back once Dev is asleep.

When he's in his PJs I send him rocketing into the living room to

kiss Mommy good night, and then he's back, running down the hallway to bounce into bed. We get the covers sorted out, I kiss him on
the cheek, and then I look in his closet and under his bed for mon-
sters. When he's satisfied that everything is safe, he snuggles down
and is almost instantly asleep. I kiss him again and then shut off the
light and leave the room.

Gillie is reading a book. 'James White called,' she says and I stop,
frozen in place. 'What?' she asks. 'What's wrong?'

'Nothing,' I say. I walk over and sit down in my chair, which faces
where we used to keep the TV. When Devon was born that was
another change we thought we'd try, quitting TV cold turkey. We
hardly watched it, but still it feels like I've given up a religion or
something. 'What did he say?'

'Not much.' Gillie is already back into her book. 'He'll phone you
again tomorrow.'

'James White?' I ask.

'James White. He said you were old friends.' And I sit and stare at
a space that used to contain a TV, wondering what on earth James
could mean by phoning me.

The next day, it's my turn to pick Devon up from daycare. If you ask
my son if he goes to daycare, he'll shake his head. 'Mrs Peterson's,'
he'll say. 'And that's daycare?' you can ask. 'Mrs Peterson's!' he'll say
again, 'Mrs Peterson's!' So, three days a week I get off early and pick
Dev up from Mrs Peterson's.

At first it was hard for us to leave Dev in the care of a stranger, but
now she feels like family. She costs a little more but comes highly recommended. Devon likes her, and we feel safe leaving him with her.

I think of these things when I drive away from Mrs Peterson's
house. And then I think of all the things you read in the paper and
remind myself that you can never be sure. I think about James
White.

I'm fixing dinner when the phone rings. Gillie answers it and then
calls, 'It's for you.' I have to wash and dry my hands, then I walk over
and she hands me the phone.

'Hello, Rob?' a voice asks.

I breathe in and then breathe out. The lid on the big pot begins to rattle. The spaghetti should go in, soon.

'Hello, James,' I say.

I'm quiet all through dinner. I know that I am, and I know that Gillie will notice, but I can't help it. I chew my food, I cut more pieces of bread. When I finally look across the table, Gillie is staring at me.

'What?' I say.

'Rob, what's wrong?'

I shake my head. 'Nothing. Nothing is wrong. I'm just not in a talkative mood.'

Gillie lets this sit for a moment, then: 'Who was on the phone?'

I put my fork on my empty plate, just so, and push my chair back from the table. 'James White. James White called.'

'The man from yesterday.'

I nod. 'Yes, the man from yesterday.'

And I know I'm doing it. I'm making Gillie pull all of this out of me, but I can't stop. I'm acting like a sullen teenager and I know I'm acting like a sullen teenager but I can't or won't stop.

But, fortunately, Gillie knows how to handle me. 'He's an old friend?' she asks.

I nod, sip from my glass of water, look at Gillie and then away, have another sip of water, and nod again. 'Yes,' I say. 'He's probably my oldest friend. My childhood best friend.'

'And?' she says, drawing the syllable out, a parent coaxing a recalcitrant child. I'm starting to feel a little ridiculous in the role I've written for myself.

'He's been transferred out here. He was in Ontario, but now he's been transferred out here.'

'He's here now?'

I nod. 'Yes, he's here now.'

'And you didn't invite him for dinner? The man has just arrived from Ontario and –'

I cut her off. 'Gillie, you don't understand. He's been transferred. He's in prison. He's a prisoner.'

She waits until we are in bed, just before we fall asleep. Devon has been sleeping for hours, the house is quiet. I've switched off the bedside lamp and kissed Gillie good night. But I can feel her lying awake beside me and I know what's coming.

'Rob,' she says, 'what did he do?'

I lie there, feeling the pillow cool at the back of my neck. I stare up into the dark, wondering how I can say this. I've been holding my breath and now I let the air escape – I don't breathe out, I don't force the air out, I just let it escape, leave my body. 'He killed a little boy,' I say. 'He raped and murdered a five-year-old boy.' And neither of us can think of anything to say after that.

We leave it for several days. We both carry on in a slightly forced, slightly brittle way. We don't talk about it. But it's something that has come into our house and won't go away, something that has become an unseen part of every moment between us.

It's Gillie who finally breaks the silence. 'They should just kill them all,' she says, and of course I know what she's talking about. 'I'm sorry, that's a horrible thing to say, but that's how I feel. They should just kill them.'

I look at her face and I see the anguish that feeling this way causes her. This is not who we are, we've never been the ones to howl for blood, to search out the easy answers. I hug her, pulling her close, feeling how tense she is.

'I know,' I say. 'I know.' And I do. When I was younger it was easier for me to be pure. I wouldn't have felt this way, then. I would have told you how violence and murder were wrong, even when done by the state. I would have laid out a series of rational and convincing arguments. A civilized man. But now I'm a husband and I'm the father of a two-year-old boy, and I don't like what I see happening in the world. And I can understand and not understand, both.

'It's not right,' Gillie is saying. 'We live in fear now, all the time. We have to worry about our kids every moment.' She draws back to look at me, and I see that she has been quietly crying. 'How can Devon have a childhood when we have to follow him around, know where he is every second? These people have made us live like that and it's *wrong*.' She's crying, but now she's angry, too. 'What kind of a world is this?' she says. 'How can it be like this?'

And I can't answer her. I don't have the words. 'Shh,' I say, pulling her into another hug. 'It's all right, everything is all right.' Even as I say these things I know that everything is not all right. And I feel like there is something lacking in me, some gap, that I can't do more to comfort her.

Gillie stands back, drying her cheeks with the back of her hand, looking at me hard. 'Rob,' she says. 'Why did he phone you? You didn't say why he phoned you.'

I look her right in the eyes; I owe her that much. 'He wants me to visit him. I'm going to go visit him, this Saturday.'

And Gillie just stands and stares at me.

I take along a map and still I get lost. They've built this place out in the country, or what used to be the country. It's starting to change now and farms are slowly becoming subdivisions, a bit of light industry. I stop at some kind of gas station that's only for trucks – a card lock, the sign says – and ask a fellow who's pumping gas into an old Ford if he can give me directions. He's never heard of the place but at least he shows me where I am on my map.

It's already been a long morning. Gillie sat and watched me eat my breakfast, sipping her cup of coffee and pointedly not speaking. She's beyond furious at me and I can't blame her. When I opened the door and turned to say goodbye, she walked over to rinse her cup in the sink. I waited while she ran the water and swished it around in the cup. She took a dish towel and carefully dried the mug, rubbing it inside and out, over and over, before placing it on the rack.

'Gillie,' I said.

She shook her head, holding the counter with both hands.

'Gillie.'

'*Don't*, Rob. Just don't.'

I released the edge of the door and rubbed the palm of my hand. 'I have to, Gillie,' I said. 'I have to do this. He was my –'

'I *know*,' she said. 'I know what he was.' She turned around. 'And I know why you have to go see him, but I don't have to like it. Rob, he killed a little boy. He's not your friend any more, he's someone who has, he's someone who has –' She stopped and I could see that she was trying not to cry. She kept swallowing, and she looked away from me for a few seconds, gathering herself.

And I should have moved toward her. There were maybe eight feet between us and I should have crossed them, then. 'I know, Gillie. It's not something I want to do, but I –'

'Just go, Rob,' she said. 'Just go.' She turned around and ran the water to wash the mug she'd just cleaned.

Pretty soon I'm in real countryside. Fields that are just beginning to be full of whatever it is that they grow here. I recognize corn, but that's about it. The rest is as complete a mystery to me as there can be. I smile at this, because I grew up here, I've spent my entire life in this part of the world and I still don't know what it is they grow on all the land. Likely it no longer matters; the real cash crop will be houses.

And I must have driven right by it, because I wind up doubling back. I'm so busy looking for what I imagine a prison to look like – lots of grey concrete, guard towers, movie detail – that I still don't think I'm at the right place even when I pull up.

I met James when I was twelve or thirteen. When, for some reason, some casual malevolence of childhood, my group of friends decided I couldn't be one of them, never would be again. The cruelty takes your breath away. And James quietly, bravely, took their place. Became my only friend when I most desperately needed him. In a way that makes no sense to me as an adult but is brightly clear to my child-self, James White saved my life. It's hard now to remember how desperate that loneliness was. And I can only pray that when it happens to Devon it is short-lived. And I'm appalled when I find myself hoping that there will be someone like James White, for him.

I can't say – the way they do in the newspapers all the time – that he was the last person you'd expect. I can't say anything one way or the other. He wasn't anything special. He was no one you'd particularly expect and he was no one you'd particularly not expect. He was just someone I knew. Who knows, maybe they've done studies, maybe that means something.

The place is so new that the lawn is still being seeded. It looks like a community centre, this one-storey building with all the brickwork, the new shrubs placed just so. I drive up and the driveway loops past what must be the front door and then leads me to a small parking lot. They haven't painted the lines yet. The dark new pavement is dotted with blobs of yellow paint, though, and I park between two of them. There isn't another car in the lot.

I still haven't seen anything that would make me think this place is a prison. The door opens in front of me, it's got one of those infrared things you see at the supermarkets, and I see the low wooden sign set in the garden with the ornamental cedars. 'Glenn Gould Facility,' it says, the letters burned into the wood. The name makes about as much sense as any dead prime minister's, I suppose. And it isn't a prison, it is a 'facility.'

There is a small reception area inside, with a man behind a desk. By now I've figured out that they're trying to avoid the look of a prison, so I'm not surprised to see he's not wearing a uniform.

'I'm Rob Bartlett,' I say. 'I'm here to visit –'

'James White,' he finishes for me. He stands and we shake hands. He tells me his name, which I immediately forget, and tells me that he's one of the staffers at Gould. 'You're right on time,' he says. 'No problems finding the place?'

I shake my head and look around. 'No,' I say, 'but I sure wasn't looking for this.'

He laughs and looks around with me. 'No, I suppose not. What do you think?'

He touches me lightly on the elbow and leads me to a door that, I notice, he opens with a plastic card, like the one the old man with the Ford used at the gas station. 'You've done a good job,' I say. 'This is nicer than most of the apartment buildings I've lived in.' He laughs, but I get the feeling he'll be tired of that joke soon.

'James is in the meeting room,' he says. 'You'll have an hour.' He reaches to open a door for me, one that doesn't have a lock in it, then stops. 'Just a formality, but you know that you mustn't give anything to James while you're here?' I nod, but he presses the point. 'I'm obliged to tell you that it's an offence to pass any material to an inmate without the knowledge and consent of the staff. Do you understand that?' I nod again, then realize that he is waiting for me to make a verbal acknowledgement. I tell him, yes, I understand, and for the first time I feel that I'm inside a prison. He opens the door.

James has been sitting on a sofa and now stands. 'Hello, Rob,' he says. He stands there, watching me. He looks like himself, he looks exactly like the man he was the last time I saw him, at least ten years ago. Maybe his hairline has moved back at the sides, but so has mine. I try to remember if he had a moustache the last time I saw him. In any case, he is now clean-shaven. He's thinner than I remember but that is all the difference I notice.

The room could be the commons of a dormitory, or the conference room of some small business. A couple of plain couches, a low coffee table, one longish wooden table with six stylish wooden chairs around it. There's a photograph of someone playing the piano, a large black-and-white print in a simple frame. I assume this is Glenn Gould.

'Hello, James,' I say. 'How are you?' I move into the room.

We talk about nothing at all. Variations of 'What ever happened to....' and 'I heard from somebody that....' The same conversations I have when I fly to visit my parents each year. The noises you make when there is nothing to be said and yet you must say something. Even so, I'm surprised when there's a knock at the door. I look at James and he shrugs. 'Hour's up,' he says, and stands.

I stand too and the door opens. James walks with me into the hallway and extends his hand. Then, as quick as a reflex, we embrace and pull apart again, embarrassed. I could get away then, escape, but before I change my mind I blurt out the thing I've come here to ask. 'James. Why did you do it?'

James doesn't blink, doesn't look away, he doesn't do anything. He cocks his head slightly, as though he's heard an odd sound from far away, and looks right at me. His face is open, honest, with the half smile he's carried all his life. 'Why did I do what?' he asks.

I turn and walk quickly away, leaving James standing next to the open door.

When the guard and I are back in the reception area I tell him I'm surprised at how few people I've seen. 'It's just new,' he says, 'so we're still filling it. Your friend James is one of the first to be transferred here.' I'm not sure if he puts any emphasis on the word 'friend'. He shakes my hand, and I can tell that he wants me to go. But I'm curious.

'So eventually it will be full?' I ask. 'With all sorts of prisoners?'

The man studies me for a second before responding. 'No,' he

says, 'this facility is only for one kind of prisoner. Only sexual offenders are incarcerated here, and only ones who have demonstrated that they aren't a risk to escape.'

I look around, as if I could take in the scope of the building from inside the room. 'Just for sex offenders?' I ask. 'There are that many?'

He laughs, a very neutral sound. 'This facility is just for the province,' he says. 'We'll have no problem filling this place up, no problem at all.'

I nod and shake his hand again. He walks me to the front door and uses his card to make the door open. I wonder how they stop someone else from using that card, it looks like it would be so easy to escape, then I figure that they must have some other system as well, something I don't know about. My car is still the only one in the lot, a small red blob in the middle of an expanse of new black tar.

Gillie is waiting for me when I get home. She opens the door while I am still parking and waits while I climb the stairs. Before I can say anything she shushes me with her hand. 'Rob,' she says, 'I want you to know that I wasn't mad at you, before.'

'I know,' I say as we go into the house. 'Me either.'

'No, I mean it. I wasn't.' She stops walking and I wonder what's coming. 'I wasn't even mad at him, at James.' Now she's looking at me, trying to make me see what she means. She reaches and grabs me by my biceps, hard. 'I was just angry at the way things are, that's all. Just angry.' She lets go of my arm. 'I guess I still am.'

I have nothing I can say to that. There is nothing for me to do but rub my arm and then go help with dinner, do the dishes, all the things that I would do anyway.

But Gillie isn't done with it. I'm trying to convince Devon that rice is good for something other than flicking onto the floor and when I turn back to Gillie I can tell that she wants to say something. She takes a bite of her squash and chews, watching me the whole time. I wait.

'So, how was it?' she finally says.

'It was OK,' I tell her. A grain of rice hits me in the side of face and Devon giggles. I wipe my face with my napkin, but I continue to

look at Gillie. 'I wasn't sure what to expect, but it turned out O K.' I
think about it. 'I don't think I'll have to go again.'

Gillie nods her head, punctuating what I'm saying. 'Could you,
you know –' she asks.

'What?'

'Could you tell. About James, could you tell?'

I reconstruct James's face in my mind, laying it over the memories
I have of that same, younger face. I imagine that I will be able to tell
differences in the man from where the two pictures don't quite coin-
cide. If I pay enough attention I'll be able to divine from the shape of
his jaw, the wrinkles around his eyes, what kind of a man he is and
whether he's always been that way.

'I don't know,' I say. 'He was just James, the way he's always been.
I don't think anybody would be able to tell.' I think about him some
more, but the image of his face blurs and fades. All I am left with is
the idea of him and I'm not sure what that idea is. But I need to tell
Gillie something, anything. 'We wear the same brand of watch. And
he's quit smoking, that was something he told me. He said it was
hard, but it's pretty well over now.' I shrug my shoulders, but there is
nothing left from the visit. 'He could have been anyone, Gillie, he
could have been anyone.' I return to my dinner and eat methodically
until it is finished.

When the water is warm but not hot, safe, I push in the plug and put
Devon in the tub. He likes to sit and splash as the tub slowly fills. I
imagine that he's delighted as the tub changes from one thing to
another: from a dry and slightly cold box to a plaything that is hot
and wet and wonderful. Something that he plays in with his daddy.

I undress, hanging my clothes on the back of the door, dropping
my socks and underwear in the laundry hamper. I'm always watching Devon out of the corner of my eye, though. All Devon knows is
that the water is his old friend, but still I watch.

I sit down on the closed lid of the toilet. Devon stops splashing
and looks at me. This is something unusual for him; usually I get
right in the tub. Instead I lean forward and sit with my elbows resting on my knees. I look down at my feet, my toenails that need cutting. I have a bruise on one calf that I don't remember. My penis

· · · 94 · · ·

rests on the cool plastic of the toilet lid, and I look at it. The cold stimulates it and with the jump of a heartbeat it grows slightly. I look ahead, at the two towels I have hung on the rack.

'Daddy!' Devon calls and I look up. 'Daddy!' he says again, and splashes the water. I lean over and twist the faucets off, but then I sit back. I rub the finger of one hand and look down.

'Daddee!!' Devon calls, wanting me in the tub, wanting me right now. His voice has changed and he knows that something is wrong, that something has changed. I sit and look down, wondering if it will be possible to be an innocent, ever again.

RIP, Roger Miller

HE HASN'T COME RIGHT OUT and said it yet, not directly any-how, but John thinks I should be moving on. We go way back, me and him, but even so.

I'm all set up in an old barn of his. John's got this two-bit farm he's busy running into the ground and off in one corner of the lower field is what's left of a barn. I hauled in an eight-foot camper some-one gave me, set it down, and I've been there ever since. I guess more time than I thought has passed, because now I'm getting the pretty strong feeling that John wants me gone.

Or his wife does, and I can't really blame her too much. Me hunk-ered down in a travel camper in a barn with no running water and no power, well, some people might object. I've been happy, though. Happy enough.

'Don't even think about it,' he said to me when I first hauled up. 'Don't even goddamn think about it.' Maybe that was when I got off to a bad start with his wife, showing up out of the blue with nothing to my name but an old camper and a bottle of Lamb's Navy Rum. John and I got the camper tucked into a dry corner of his barn and then sat and killed the bottle. Maybe that was what got between me and his wife. This was two years ago. It doesn't seem that long, but John tells me it is.

I watch the stars a lot. I'll sit out behind my barn, facing nothing but scrub forest and field so long fallow it's gone back to whatever it was before, and watch the stars move around. It gets so dark that it's like sitting in a big sack of nothing at all, the only light the end of my cigarette. I sit with a glass of rum and a smoke, watching the stars, looking for comets or whatever, and there's nothing like it.

You can hear the coyotes. People will try to tell you they're wolves, but they're only coyotes. You can even see the odd one, if there's a moon and you're lucky and quick, slinking across an open space, headed from somewhere to somewhere else.

I had a dog once, Annie, an old hound of some kind. I bought a shotgun off this old fellow, a tiny little gun, a .410, and the dog sort of came with the deal. I didn't want her at the time but he pressed her on me. He couldn't get around so well any more, that was why he was selling the .410, and he didn't think it was right to keep a dog that he couldn't run. Anyway, she used to bark back at the coyotes, howl back at them. That wasn't here, of course. That was a while back, somewhere else. But all memories seem to happen in the same place, if you let them.

Monday is John's day to drive to town for supplies. He turns off his road and onto the secondary at seven-thirty in the morning, like clockwork, so I have to set off by seven at the latest. It takes me almost half an hour to walk to the road and then a little way along it. That way, I'm walking to town and if John decides to stop for me, well, that's fine. So far he has, every time, but this way we each have the option.

The truck stops, just ahead of me, the engine ticking from not being warmed up properly. I walk up, throw my sack in the box, and climb in the cab with John. He puts it in gear and pulls out, shaking his head. I wait for him to say something but he doesn't, so I don't either.

We make it all the way into town without a word, until John pulls the truck up and shuts it off. Then, just before I can open the door, he asks, 'You making it O K?'

Yeah, I tell him, sure. I'm making it fine. He nods, like I've answered a real question, something he's been wondering about. Then he reaches into his shirt pocket, where he'd keep his cigarettes if he still smoked, and passes me a folded twenty-dollar bill.

'Here,' he says, 'don't let Gail know about this.' Before I can turn him down, or before I can think of how to say thank you, he's hopped out of his truck and walking away.

I don't think I ever even fired the .410. Maybe once, just to see what kind of kick it had, but likely not. The old guy I got it from used it for grouse, used it for years until his body got so worn down he couldn't hack it any more. You could tell he was crazy about hunting and all busted up by not being able to do it any more. I had to sit around half the day listening to his stories, drinking his watery coffee, before I could get out of there. It seemed like the right thing to do though, spend some time with the old guy. It was right at the end that he brought old Annie out, told me how he couldn't run her any more. There were honest-to-God tears running down his face when I drove away with that dog.

I take care of my laundry. I drop by the fuel company and arrange to have more propane delivered. They'll do it, but they tell me they can only carry me one more month unless I make good on my bill. 'You say hello to John for me,' the fuel man says. 'He's a good man.' Meaning that some of us aren't, I suppose. I tell him I will.

I buy a few tins of this and that at the grocery, and a can of loose tobacco. With John's twenty and what's left of my money I've got enough for a bottle of Lamb's and I pick that up last. It's criminal what they charge for it now. The clerk watches me from the second I walk in the door, all the way down the aisle to the rum, and back again. Like I'm going to start stuffing bottles in my pockets and make a run for it. He watches my hands shake as I count out the change for him, and doesn't say a word as he hands me my bottle in a paper bag. I thank him politely and leave. He has no idea who I am or what I'm all about and I'm not about to tell him. He can think what he wants.

In the truck on the way back I notice that I'm humming under my breath, over and over, the same song.

Trailer for sale or rent,
Rooms to let – fifty cents.
No phone, no pool, no pets;
I ain't got no cigarettes.

'What is that, anyway?' I ask John.
'What's what?' he says, the first thing he's said since we set off.
'That song: "Trailer for sale or rent". Who sings that? I've had it buzzing around my head all day.'
John thinks about it. '"It's 'King of the Road",' he tells me. 'Roger Miller.'

Roger Miller. Right, I remember now. I remember hearing it come over the radio, announced the way they do with his name. Years ago. 'I sure like that song,' I say. 'What's Roger Miller up to these days?'

'Dead, I think,' says John. 'A couple of years ago.'

So I've got a dead man's song rattling around my skull.

'Imagine that,' I say. 'You think I would have heard about it.' John just grunts. 'You'd think someone would have told me,' I say. I stare out the window all the way back, feeling vaguely sad about the whole deal.

The old man, he claimed that a .410 gave the birds a sporting chance. Most yahoos, they charge around the bush with heavy artillery, usually a 12-gauge. But a .410, a little gun like that, evened things up, if only a little. He told me all this when he sold me the gun and threw in a box or two of shells, skinny little shotgun shells about as big around as your finger. Course, he told me, the real joy comes from walking around the bush country, you and your dog, just being out there. It didn't matter if you got your grouse or whatever, or not, the point was you and your dog being out there. Which brought him around to Annie.

The reason I wanted to buy the .410 was I thought it would be the right thing to do. I still had my little boy then. I had this idea in my head that a boy should grow up with memories of fall days spent bird hunting with his father. God only knows where I got that from. So I wanted to get a little gun, something my boy would be able to at least hold, get the feel of. One that, when he fired it, wouldn't send him flying. That was why I bought it, so I could have this perfect picture of me and him, the two of us in this memory.

'I ever tell you about my boy?' I ask John. He's driven me all the way down to my barn, to drop me off before turning around and heading up to his house.

John shakes his head. 'I don't think so. Not that much, anyhow.'

'Well,' I say, 'you come on down for a drink some time. Any time you want, you come on down.'

'I'll do that,' says John. 'I'll have to do that some time.'

'Any time at all. You know where to find me.'

It looks to rain that night so I pull my chair inside the barn. The barn is missing patches of roof, lengths of plank siding from the walls, but it still keeps its insides mostly dry. There's a wild feeling to it, though. When you're in it you can still see out, still feel the cold and the mist from the rain, so it's a bit like you're not inside and you're not outside. I sit and sip at my rum, and I'm still humming that damn song. For some reason I'm all sad that Roger Miller is dead, has been dead for a couple of years and I didn't know a thing about it. And, try as I might, all I can remember is that one little snatch of the song. This is something I used to hear all the time, probably used to sing to myself, and now it's almost gone. I keep trying though. I have the crazy idea that I owe it to old Roger, that the least I can do for him is try to remember his song.

While she was in the process of leaving me, moving from room to room packing up clothes, knickknacks, our son's toys, I sat in my chair and smoked my cigarette. Not saying a word, not moving a muscle. She didn't say anything either, just moved from one room to another, packing up. If I saw two people act like that on TV, it would look pretty funny. Two stubborn people, not saying a word. When she was done she herded my boy to the door. It opened and then closed and that was the last I saw of them. I poured another glass of rum, rolled another cigarette, and sat there in my chair. I didn't even turn my head to see the door close.

I don't know what happened to the .410. The last I remember having it was when Annie got really sick. No, what she got was old. So old I had to boost her up into the cab of the truck I had then, hoist her back out again. She got so bad that she'd walk five or six feet, then stop, panting, resting up for the next five or six.

A man's got to shoot his own dog. I'd heard that, I guess I believed it, and that's what I set out to do. I took Annie and the .410 and a shovel and drove out in the bush. I hoisted her down out of the cab and then walked into the scrub a ways. I dug a good hole and then went back for her. She wasn't ten feet from the truck, her head down, looking beat to hell. When she heard me come out of the bush, though, her whip of a tail started slapping against her flank. She was a good old girl, was Annie.

I had to pick her up and carry her in. I set her down, right next to the fresh hole, and picked up the .410. Annie didn't even look up at me, just stood there, like she was waiting. And I picked up the gun and aimed it at her head, knowing I was doing the right thing, that I was doing right by her. But I couldn't do it, even if it was the right thing to do.

I swore at myself all the way into town to the vet's. I gave him twenty dollars and told him I'd bring him the rest if he'd just do this for me. He asked me if I wanted to stay with her while he did it, but I couldn't. I guess I let Annie down, but I couldn't stay there. I'll admit it: I was crying like a baby when I drove away from there, howling like a baby with its heart broken.

Maybe I left the .410 in the woods, beside that hole. I didn't have any use for it, so maybe I just left it there. And I still owe that vet the rest of the money. That's going back some time now and I bet he's forgotten, but if I'm ever back that way I'll try to pay him what I owe.

When I think of my boy, he's seven years old. He's wearing a striped T-shirt, red and blue, and he's just standing there, looking square at me. I last saw him when he was seven, and this is going on ten or eleven years now, maybe more, so I know he won't look like that any more. And he never had a striped T-shirt that I know of. Memory is funny that way, filling in details, colours, T-shirts that never were. Maybe I picked up that picture from some TV show. I still think of running into him, though, meeting him on the street. And he's always that same age, and he's always wearing that same damn T-shirt. It's like I can't imagine him any other way, like that's all I've got left of him, this memory that more than likely never happened. I wonder how he thinks of me, if he does. How I look to him in his memories when he thinks of me. I don't know if I want him to or not.

I'm sitting, waiting to catch a glimpse of a coyote, when I hear footsteps crunching on the gravel and dried grass. I check to see that there's still some rum left at the bottom of the bottle, so I'll have something to offer John. But it's not John who walks up and stands there but his wife, Gail. John must have told her where to find me, since I don't think she's ever been down to this end of their farm, at least not in the two years I've been here.

I'm a little surprised but still manage to get up out of my chair and offer it to her. Even at the bottom of a dead field, sitting with no power or water, half in the bag from Lamb's Navy, I like to think I keep my manners.

And Gail keeps hers. She thanks me for the chair and sits down, like that's why she came by, to sit and wait for the coyotes with me.

I fetch my other chair, the one I've been saving for John if he drops by, and pull that up. I know what's coming, I know that Gail's going to give me my walking papers, but I also know that there's nothing I can do about it.

'How are you doing?' she asks me. 'Are you making it OK out here?' Making it OK. So she and John have been talking about me.

She sounds genuinely concerned, though. She's a nice lady, after all, and she sounds worried for me. 'I'm fine,' I say. 'I'm making it. I'm not making much of it, but I'm making it.' I say this last bit as a joke and she's nice enough to laugh along with me, say: well, good, then.

My glass is empty and I wipe it clean on the tail of my shirt. 'Can I pour you some rum?' I ask, holding up the glass and what's left of the bottle.

'Thank you,' she says, 'but just a little.' So I do, splashing a couple of fingers into the glass for her. I keep the bottle, since I don't have another glass. There's not much left covering the bottom and I don't think Gail will object to me nipping at what's left. I'm not hiding anything from her.

She sips at her rum and looks out over the field. I'd expected her to mention that it was awfully strong, or that she usually took mix, something like that, but she doesn't. She hunkers down in her chair and sips at her rum like she's been doing this all her life.

'John's worried about you,' she says. 'It's hard for him to say things straight out, but he's worried about you.'

'Well,' I say, 'John doesn't have to –'

'*I'm* worried about you,' she says.

I don't have an answer for that one. Instead I take a pull at the bottle and squint out into the dark, pretending to myself that I saw something move.

'Do you know how long you've been here?' I don't say anything, because I know what's coming. 'It's coming up to three years you've been sitting out here, living on rum and cigarettes, and....' She trails off. I should probably say something, tell her that I'll be pulling out, it's something I had planned to tell her, I'll be leaving early next week, tell her something like that. But I don't. I roll a cigarette and light it, take another mouthful of rum from the bottle. Rum and cigarettes, like she said.

'John tells me that you were married. That you had a little boy.'

I nod, not looking at her. 'That was a long time ago,' I say. 'A long time.'

'Oh,' she says. Then, 'Have you seen him lately? Your boy, I mean.'

I shake my head. 'Not in a little while,' I say. 'Listen, Gail.'

'Yes.'

'Have you ever heard of Roger Miller, the singer?'

She thinks about it. 'No, I don't think so. Why?'

'He sang "King of the Road"? Roger Miller?'

'No, I don't think so,' she says again. 'Is it important?'

No, I tell her, it's not important. Just something I was wondering about. About how someone can be alive in your mind, you might not even know who they are, or their name, but they're alive in your mind, them and their song. And then, poof, you hear that they're not alive. That they're dead and have maybe been dead for a long time. It's a strange way to be thinking, I tell her, but it's the kind of thing that rattles around my brain. I'm aware that while I'm telling her all this I'm talking faster and faster, trying to use words to fill up all the space in the barn, in my head, in the world.

'What was your boy's name?' she asks me. Like she hasn't paid any attention to all the things I've just been saying. And I'm scared, I'm honest-to-God scared to death that she's going to make me tell her, when I see a flash of movement, a quick blur of shadow against some other shadows halfway across the field.

'You see that,' I say, pointing. 'A coyote just ran across. If we wait we'll likely see some more.'

'Coyotes?' she says, her voice a little excited and a little disbelieving.

'You can hear them a lot of the time,' I say. 'Howling.'

'I thought that was just some dogs at the next farm,' she says, 'barking at the moon.'

I shake my head. 'You can hear dogs answer back at them sometimes, but first you'll hear the coyotes.' I pull at the bottle, but it's empty now. 'I used to have an old hound that would listen for them with me. We'd sit out and listen to the yipping and howling and at some point she'd decide to join in. It was like she was letting them know she was there, and she understood, but she wouldn't be joining them. You know?'

Gail finishes her drink and puts the glass down next to the empty bottle. She reaches over and touches me, lightly, on my arm. 'Listen,' she says, 'I think you need some help. We, John and I, we'd like to give you some if you'll –'

I shake off her hand and half turn my chair so she can't see that I'm crying, tears running down my cheeks like I'm a little girl. 'Her name was Annie,' I say. 'She's dead now, Annie.' I reach for the bottle and then remember that it's all used up. 'I miss that old dog. I sure do.'

Deer

THE TAIL END OF the news finishes and while I'm up turning off the television Cathy is at the window again. She peeks out, no more than a casual glance, and then she rearranges the curtains, tugging them this way and that, making everything straight.

'Don't worry,' I say.

She lets the curtain fall back and smiles at me. 'I'm not worried.' She stands there, still holding a corner of the material. 'I'm just –'

'Worried.' I go over and put my arm on her shoulder. 'He's a big boy,' I say. 'He doesn't need his mother to look out for him any more. Let's go to bed.' The hardest thing about being the parent of a sixteen-year-old? Doing nothing at all. Cathy doesn't move.

'We'll leave the light on,' I say. 'He'll be home soon.'

'You go ahead,' Cathy says. 'I'm not all that sleepy. Maybe I'll stay up for a while.' Maybe I'll stay up for a while, the anthem of mothers of teenagers everywhere. I kiss her on the forehead and leave her to her crossword puzzle and her fears, no less real because they are unlikely.

'Bill, wake up. Wake up.' She's shaking me by my shoulder and it takes a few seconds to figure out what's going on.

'What time is it?' I ask.

'It's David,' she says. 'It's David. Something's wrong.' And I very calmly get out of bed and put on my robe, willing myself not to think, to have no imagination whatsoever.

We walk together back to the living room. David is standing against the wall but there is no blood, there are no police. My son is safe and now I can breathe, now I can allow myself to open back up to the world.

'There's something wrong with him,' Cathy says. 'Bill, there's something wrong with him.'

David is leaning against the wall and when I say his name he startles a little and then turns his head to look at me. His eyes are wide and his face is blank, worse than blank, his face is soft, flaccid, as if something has drained out of it. His eyes move through me, caught by something, then wander back to stare in wonder at my face, my hair, the wall behind me. One of his hands moves and he looks down to discover it. He stares at it, Cathy and I forgotten.

'Bill,' says Cathy, 'Bill.' And we stand there, two people in their dressing gowns, two adults, two parents.

Cathy thinks it's funny and a little bit wild that I smoked some pot in college. She has this image of me, painted from my occasional stories: long hair and jean jacket, the young rebel. This has built up, over the years, and is now a small running joke between us. Willie the Hippie. We laugh about what I was, how far I've come. We get a real kick out of it, to tell you the truth.

And, of course, what we remember is a complete fiction.

When I was twenty and still thought I knew everything, I got in over my head with a number of things, one in particular. To put it into what seems now almost abstract terms, I found myself addicted to heroin. And, eventually, I realized that I couldn't go on the way I was.

I took a ferry to Vancouver Island and then a series of bus rides and hitch-hikes north, up the coast. I wound up in a small mill town, walked in the front door of the mill, and started work the next day. That was back when there were jobs. That was back when a young guy could do something like that, could always find something. I don't know what they do now. It worries me sometimes that David might not have that one last chance.

I worked in the machine room of the Tahsis Co. Pulp Mill and went outside every hour to throw up in the snow. I told the foreman I had the flu. It took a week and then I was mostly better.

Things fade, and I now have very few memories left of that time. On occasion I find it difficult to believe that I was the one involved, that I was the one who did those things. On those occasions I rub my left arm, the smooth white skin on the inside of my elbow where there used to be a vein. So it's gone, and possibly much more, but things turned out OK for me. Sometimes luck figures more than we can know, I believe.

And yet there is something I regret leaving behind. I don't even know if I have a name for it, but it's gone nonetheless. Every gain somewhere is a loss somewhere else. I can never tell Cathy any of this.

'Go to bed, Cathy,' I say. 'Everything is going to be fine.' I speak in a calm voice, low and even. A father's voice. I don't know if David can understand me, but I am talking for him.

Cathy is not a stupid person. This is not a part of her experience, and yet it is. This is something that parents think about. This is one of the worries that start almost immediately and, I guess, never end. Her voice is low, calm, and she too looks as though something has drained away. 'It's not supposed to be like this,' she says. 'It wasn't supposed to be like this. Not us.'

David is looking at her, now. He's studying her face the way you see people in museums and art galleries do, peering at every detail, seeking out every hidden scrap of meaning.

'Yes,' I say. And David is looking at me, his eyes wide and black, terrified. His eyes are the only part of his face that is alive, and they are huge and liquid, and he is afraid of me.

I would leave town, almost every weekend. I'd started to make friends, become good at my job, settle. And so I would leave the barracks I lived in, afraid that it was becoming home. Looking back, now, I can't begin to imagine the desperation.

Because the thing that I can't ever tell Cathy is that I chose to do what I did. Now we watch movies or read magazine articles and words like compulsion, possession, are the ones used. And they may be the right ones, I don't know. What I do know is that I always had a choice, I could always do one thing or another, like electing to turn left or right at a corner. And my choices might have been limited, and some might have been much harder than others, but they were still choices. And how do you tell your wife something like that?

Driving back at night, tired after two days of hiking, or reading, or driving, I'd drive through the dark forest on the way back to my mill town. And a funny thing would happen. The shadows of the trees, and my fatigue, and the complete loneliness of being the only human being on the road, made me see things. The deer there were as common as cats and the thing I was most afraid of was hitting one. And I'd see them, I'd see deer at the edge of the road and I'd be just at the point of jumping on my brakes, twisting the steering wheel, when I'd see that it was a tree, or a shadow, I'd see that the thing I was desperate to avoid was just my imagination. My fears come to life.

But it happened. I think I must have been in that trance you can fall into when you've been driving too long, with not enough sleep. You find that your eyes are still open, and you are still looking, seeing, but your focus has shifted from the road to the glass of your windshield. You no longer are connected to the body that is driving the car but are staring at chips in the glass, motes of dust, nothing at all.

I braked as hard as I could, and swerved across the road. The deer, staring into the bright lights that were hunting it down, first froze and then darted in front of me. The impact took so long to come that I first thought I'd been spared.

When I got out I saw that it was no bigger than a large German shepherd, there under the fender of my car. It lay there, its chest rising and falling in short, rasping breaths. Blood was running from its nose. I remember that, in the glare of my headlights, I didn't know what the blood was at first, it looked so dark, so viscous. The deer's left front leg was twisted up beside its head, the jagged edge of a bone tearing through the skin. In the seconds I took to realize all of this, the deer must have either gone into shock or come out of it, because it began to scream.

I walked to the back of the car and opened the trunk. I had to search for what I was looking for, tossing aside clothes, books, things of no value, but finally I found the tire iron underneath the spare. When I picked it up it was scabby with rust and dirt, and I tried to rub it clean on the sleeve of my jacket. When I walked back to the deer it was still screaming, but it stopped when I touched it. I placed my left hand on its neck, almost a caress, and the deer looked at me. Its eyes were wide, molten with terror. Its eyes were black, and human, and looking right at me.

I lead Cathy to the hallway. 'Go to bed,' I say. She nods, but I'm not sure that she's heard me. 'Go to bed,' I say again. 'He'll be all right. I'll sit with him.'

She looks at me, and we both know, I think, that I don't have any answers for her, any more than she has specific questions. I kiss her forehead and tell her the things you say, saying them just as much for me as for her.

'I want to stay up,' she says.

'No, it's better that you don't. Just one of us is better. He just needs to sit quietly.' I look back to make sure David is OK and see him opening and closing his hand, staring at it, captivated.

Cathy says it again, but her voice is soft, fading; she nods and walks to the bedroom door. She turns and opens her mouth, then closes it again. 'He'll be fine,' I say. 'I'll wake you if anything happens.'

'Yes. Yes,' Cathy says. 'Wake me then.' The door closes on her, on me. And I am filled with an overwhelming sadness at the way things are and the way things should and should not be. I walk back to be with David.

I seat David. That's an expression I've used often but never like this. I guide him to a chair and then lightly press down on his shoulders so that he sits. Like you would with a dog, like you see people do with very old people and very young children. I seat David and then I tell him that everything is going to be all right. I leave him then, to go to the kitchen. I select a paper filter and insert it in the coffee maker. I spoon out grounds from the white tin with the red lid that we've always kept just to one side. I walk over to the sink and run a pot full of water to make my coffee. I do all these things, all these normal things, and I do them as if for the first time. I pour the water into the machine and walk toward the living room, stopping just before I go through. I walk back and flick the switch that I've forgotten and then I do walk into the living room, back to my son, upset with myself for almost forgetting to switch on the machine.

I worked for a year and then I came back. I came back and I met Cathy, I finished university, I became a father. I work as a comptroller at a medium-sized transportation firm, I've been married for eighteen years, and I have a son who turns sixteen in three months. I can look back on my life and know things, the way I know what year the Armada sailed against England, or why ice occupies more space than water, but that is all. I know things, but I've only ever been this age, I've only ever been the me I am now.

We sit, he and I. I sip my coffee, knowing that I'll need it. I think to myself that at some point, likely hours from now, my son and I will be, if only for a moment, alike. Not able to sleep and not really awake, either. Maybe we'll talk then, though I don't really know what either of us will have to say. All I can hope is that when he looks back on all this, having his father sitting near him sipping coffee at three o'clock in the morning will make some sort of difference.

It seems to me that there's been a tiny hiccup between our generations. That, instead of moving forward, things have looped back. David wears tie-dyed shirts and listens to the Grateful Dead. He wears his hair long in that way young boys do, the way I did – short hair overgrown, still retaining the essence of what it once was, who this person still is. When I look at David I could be seeing myself.

And he now does drugs, of course. And do I feel any better or worse about that, having done so myself? What should I tell him? That I'm not ready to be a father yet, that I'm not sure I can play the role that I'm forced to?

I get another cup of coffee. While I'm up I pour a small glass of orange juice and bring it for David. 'David,' I say, 'David.' He turns, then, and looks at me. He opens his mouth, closes it, and then opens it again, trying to find something he has lost. 'It's O K,' I say. 'This is for you, if you get thirsty. If you get thirsty, it will be right here. O K?' David looks at the orange juice, staring at it until I realize I've been forgotten. I sit and sip at my coffee and try to imagine what he sees. I see the froth on top of the liquid, the beads of water like jewels climbing the sides of the glass. I think that this one glass contains the most intense colour in the room, in the world.

But then I leave it, drink my coffee, and open the paper. I'd like to turn on the radio, but know that silence is best. In a few hours David will be better. Maybe we'll talk then. Maybe we will have things to tell one another, things that we can both almost understand. And then I'll put on one more pot of coffee and it will be time for me to go to work. And in a world as large and confused as this one, I'll know that, sometimes, the most you can hope for is to sit up with your son, just the two of you sitting.

The King of Siam

WHEN I WAS SIXTEEN years old my father decided, a few months before he left for good, that we should spend some time together. I didn't know and likely didn't care that he would be leaving. I don't think that he knew himself, so you can't really read anything into his sudden decision to get to know me.

We were eating dinner, the three of us, early because Dad was going to the track and the first race was at six-thirty. I think my mother had long stopped worrying about what my father did or when he did it. He was like some very small-scale natural disturbance, a sudden hailstorm, a clogged drain in the sink, something you dealt with and then completely forgot. Nothing personal, nothing to get excited about.

The idea seemed to come to him in mid-chew. His fork hovered in front of his face, empty, waiting to scoop up more of whatever it was we were eating, and then he sat back and placed the fork on his plate. He finished chewing and, looking at a spot precisely between me and my mother, said, 'Maybe I'll take the boy with me tonight.' He turned his head to my mother, to me, and returned to his meal. 'That OK with you, Gary?' he asked, his mouth full again.

My turn to look at my mother, who showed nothing. 'Sure,' I said, 'I guess so.'

'Good,' my father said, 'good.' He wiped his plate with a piece of bread and pushed back from the table. 'We'd better get going, then. We don't want to miss the first race, do we?'

'No,' I said, 'we don't want to miss the parade to post.'

My father laughed. "We don't want to miss the parade to post," he repeated, mimicking me. 'What do you know, the boy's been paying attention to his old man. The kid's learned a thing or two from his old man.'

We took the bus. The Silver Limo, my dad called it. He'd sold our old Ford a while before and now made a big to-do about the benefits of being a bus-rider. I'd heard it all before and was embarrassed to have him say it again, especially since we all knew why he'd sold the car. There was no stopping him.

'Pick a man up, drop him right off, no fuss and no muss, eh Gary? Like the King of Fucking Siam and his Number One Son. Can't be beat.'

'Right,' I said. 'Number One,' I said. The bus had started out mostly empty but now as it rattled along Hastings Street it began to fill. Men got on, sometimes two or three together, but more often one at a time. Chinese, white, mostly older but some looking almost as young as me – you could tell that we were all headed to the same place. Almost all squinted at folded newspapers, making little notes in the margins with stubby pencils and Bic pens all scarred up with tooth marks.

'Where's ours?' I asked, nodding my head at the racing forms.

My dad laughed. 'Hold your horses, Ace. All in good time.' He leaned in to me, whispering. 'These yokels all think they're on to something. You stick with your old man, he'll show you what's what.' He looked up and down the aisle, not bothering to hide his contempt. 'Yokels,' he said again, louder. No one looked up.

We poured off the bus when it pulled up across from the PNE grounds. I'd been to the PNE before, of course, but only in the day-time and back when I was a kid. Now, trooping across the fair-grounds with this crowd of men, joining streams that came from other directions, all headed towards the gates of Ex Park (as my father called it; I saw now, in concrete letters above the turnstiles, that we were entering Exhibition Park), I might have been in a totally different city.

A city where everyone moved just a little bit faster than you were used to. I'd noticed us picking up speed as we walked from the bus, the whole crowd surging forward like everyone in it knew he was just that much late for something. Now my Dad paid for us both to enter and we rushed with the rest of the men into the Ex.

Dad pulled up short in front of a little kiosk. 'OK, *now* we buy the forms,' he said. He laid a dollar bill down and the man in the kiosk handed him a racing form and another paper, this one printed on yel-low newsprint. He also gave Dad a stubby little pencil, like the ones

I'd seen on the bus. I didn't catch the price of the papers, but the pencil was three cents.

'Why not bring a pen from home?' I asked.

My father looked at the pencil, then at me as if I'd asked why the sky is blue and the dirt brown and not the other way around. 'It has to be one of these,' he said. 'That's the way you do it. Come on.'

We charged off again. We passed through a big room, the size of a barn. Nothing but bare concrete floor and walls, one wall made up of a row of little booths, the betting wickets, each with a short line of bettors already waiting. Men clustered around scribbling in their forms or looking up at the TVs that hung from concrete pillars. One set of TVs showed the names and numbers of the horses that would run in the first race, while another showed the empty track. My dad didn't even slow down but kept us rushing right through this room.

We went through a big set of glass doors to the outside, where I saw the track for the first time. I didn't see much of it, and I didn't see any horses, because we immediately went through another set of glass doors and down a flight of concrete steps. Even before the smell of stale beer hit me I could tell we were in a bar.

My father led me to an empty table and we sat down. The table, one of about twenty in the room, was round with a white Arborite surface. The chairs were metal, looked like they were meant to be stacked, and uncomfortable.

'Um, Dad,' I said, hunched over the table and not looking around. 'You know I'm only sixteen, right?'

I don't think he heard. He was twisted in his chair, facing the bar at the other end of the room. A couple of men my father's age or older leaned against it, talking. Each wore an open red vest over his white shirt and big belly. Neither of them looked at us.

'Yo!' my father called, holding an arm in the air. He waved his hand with its thumb tucked in, four fingers spread, and called again. 'Yo, how about some service here?'

The men didn't appear to hear or see us, but one of them went behind the bar and started pouring beer. When he'd covered a tray with full glasses he came out from behind the bar, picked up the tray, and began going from table to table, setting glasses down whenever someone jerked a finger or nodded a head at him.

We were his last stop. He set two glasses down in front of my father and then waited, not really looking at me but not not looking either. His face and neck with its rolls of fat were shiny with sweat.

'It's O K,' my father said, 'he's with me.'

This seemed to have no effect on the man, either good or bad. He stood there.

'He's my boy,' my father said. 'Old enough to have a couple with his old man, don't you think?'

The man stood impassive for a few more seconds, then shrugged and placed two glasses in front of me. My father handed him a two-dollar bill and held his hand out, palm up, waiting for his change. The man just grunted at him, then turned and headed back to the bar. 'Asshole,' my father muttered, quietly. Then he called out, 'Keep the change!'

The man stopped in his tracks, turned, and for a moment, a sign flicking on and then quickly off again, he smiled. I had the idiotic realization that his teeth were better than you would expect, a really nice-looking smile in fact, and then he turned again and returned to the bar and his fellow waiter, who hadn't moved.

'Cheers,' my father said, and tilted a glass at me. I picked up one of my glasses and tilted it back at him. 'Um, cheers,' I said. I took a sip and put the glass back down. I'd had beer before, of course, and might have liked it. This was different, though. Practically flat and with a strong soapy taste, as if the glasses hadn't been rinsed well enough. My father didn't notice. He drank half of the glass down in one long swallow, his jaw moving as though he were chewing the beer. He stopped, winked at me over the glass, and then finished it off. 'Now, *that* hits the spot,' he said. He poured the dregs from the empty glass into his second beer and set the empty down near the edge of the table. I saw that the glasses had white lines painted on them, about a finger's width below the rim. That evening, as I watched my father drink beer after beer and always pour the last of the old into the new, the beer would rise above that white line but never overflow the rim. He did it with an ease and what I'd now have to call grace. It was the only time I saw my father be really good at something. 'Drink up,' he said, holding his fresh glass. 'Drink up.'

With two fresh beers in front of my father and me still trying to sip at my soapy first one, we opened the racing forms. My father showed me how each race was handicapped on its own page, with all the information for all the horses laid out there. Columns and columns of tiny numbers that gave the horse's racing history, how old it was, how much weight it carried, whether it ran better on a firm or muddy course. All of this and more, much more, laid out in tiny print for us to use in forecasting the race.

Though I soon saw that my father had a simple system. He'd scan the page of intricate detail, mumbling to himself, making scratches with his red pencil. Then, when he'd gone through the ritual, he'd see what the experts had recommended. The gold paper had their picks, along with comments like: 'First start ... bred for speed ... merits close look' or 'Long odds in season debut, was wide into first turn, recovered to beat half the field ... rates upset chance.' Which sounded a lot like the horoscopes my mother swore by and my father scorned. But the horse horoscope also had someone named 'Old Sam' and someone named 'Mister Gold' who picked the three winners for each race. My father's system was to see where these two agreed and then bet that horse. Even as a sixteen-year-old I could see that as a system it wasn't much.

I went with my father to bet the first race. You couldn't make the bets from where we were drinking the beer, you couldn't even see the track. We climbed up the stairs and went through the two sets of doors back into the big concrete room. My father lined up to bet two dollars on the number five horse, Billy Boy, to win. We collected the slip of paper with the bet recorded on it, then returned to our seats in the bar. We watched the race on a black and white TV that hung from the ceiling. My father didn't seem to feel one way or the other when Billy Boy came in fifth or sixth.

'I'm going to walk around,' I told my father. 'Go look at the horses.'

'Sure, sure. Check out the talent for me, that's the secret.' The waiter set two more beer in front of my father. When he reached out to pick a dollar bill off the table, my father's hand darted out and grabbed him by the wrist. 'Hey, I pay for a full glass of beer.' The beer in one of the glasses didn't quite come up to the white line, and my father let go of the waiter and tapped at it with his index finger.

The waiter, the one with the surprising smile, grunted and poured a splash of beer from the last glass on his tray. 'That's more like it,' my father said. The waiter just blinked at my father and drank off the rest of the glass in one huge gulp. He scooped up my father's dollar and headed back to the bar. I left.

I walked down through the clots of people to the rail at the edge of the track. The ground the horses ran on was dirt, loose dirt like potting soil, and you could see the marks from all the hooves. One horse and its jockey were standing all alone at a little podium near the finish line. A man walked up, flashed a picture, and walked away. The jockey jumped down from the horse and he too walked away while someone else led the horse off to wherever it was supposed to go. The jockey was even smaller than you'd expect, smaller than any adult I'd ever seen. The only thing I really noticed about him were his boots. I guess they were supposed to look good at a distance, across the track on the back of a horse. Up close they looked like doll's boots, cheap ones with broken-down ankles, made of shiny black vinyl. Something that only looks good from far away.

I hung around until the next race, about twenty-five minutes. First I just sort of wandered around, looking at people, trying to hear what they were talking about. Mostly it was just like on the bus coming here, as if bus after bus exactly like ours had filled the place up. I half expected to see two or three sets of me and my dad wandering round.

Finally the horses came out, each one walking beside some kind of trainer horse, maybe a friend, if horses have friends. So these pairs of horses walked around the track, giving everyone a look at them. Then the real racehorses all lined up, down at the start, loaded into a big green metal gate of some kind. A bell rang and all the horses came charging along, rounded the corner and mostly disappeared, almost out of sight. You could still see them, but it was hard to tell which was which and they were so far away that almost no one cared, anyway. But then they came charging around the far corner, down by where they'd started from, and people started to get interested again. The horses thundered down the straightaway and that was that, the race was over. Then I got to see the winning horse and jockey have their picture taken, and the jockey walk away in his little doll's boots, the same as before. I went back to the bar.

My dad had more beer in front of him, of course. He also had his arm around a woman who was now sitting at our table. I shouldn't have been too surprised at that but I was. Even with all the things that had happened in our lives, this wasn't something I thought I'd see my father do. I didn't show it though, just walked over and sat down.

My father leaned close and winked at me. 'Gary, I want you to meet a friend of mine. This is Shirley.' He winked again.

'Pleased,' Shirley said and held out her hand. She was my mother's age, or close enough, with badly permed hair and too much make-up. She was smoking a cigarette and when she left it in the ashtray to shake my hand I could see the thick grease smudge from her lipstick on its butt, red on white. I stared at her. I think I was hoping she was some kind of blonde bombshell, this woman with my father's arm around her, some stunner against whom my father had no chance. But she wasn't, she wasn't at all. I suppose some kind of loyalty to my mother tinted my view but, as I watched my father nuzzle at her ear, which she either ignored or somehow failed to notice, I could not imagine what he was thinking.

'Pleased,' she said again. I shook her hand and she smiled at me. She had a smear of lipstick on one of her front teeth and I could see that she was already very drunk. She was drinking beer out of a wine glass. I watched as she finished the small glass and then, with the same practised grace I'd seen in my father, refilled it from one of the regular glasses. She sipped from the wine glass and caught me staring at her. 'It's more ladylike,' she said, holding the glass by its stem in front of her face. The smear of lipstick was still there.

'Uh huh,' I said, not sure what she wanted from me.

'Some people think it's stupid. Some people don't think it's ladylike, they think it's ... stupid.' She took a tiny, elegant drink and waited.

For once in my life I knew what to do. 'You can't worry about what people think,' I said. She nodded, still waiting. 'The hell with them,' I said, 'I don't think it's stupid. I think it's ... nice.' And it might have been a lie as I said it, but it became the truth the moment it left my lips.

She smiled and put down the glass. 'You'll do,' she said. She leaned over and kissed me on the cheek. 'You'll do.'

More beer arrived. I managed to finish my first glass and pour its dregs into my second. Neither my father nor Shirley noticed. Shirley had started calling my father, whose name was William, Wayne. That was the only notice she seemed to take of him, except to occasionally pull his fingers away from groping at her breast. So the three of us sat there, me sipping at my beer, Shirley holding her wine glass and seeming to notice nothing, and my father, hunched over almost sideways, pawing at Shirley's breast. I watched him stick his tongue out and poke it in her ear, not just nibble at the lobe the way he had been, but stick his tongue into the hole of her ear. I felt sick.

'Dad,' I said. 'Dad, do you remember when I was a kid and we'd go on picnics, you, me, and Mom? Dad?' He took no notice of me. His hand was fully under Shirley's blouse now, cupped over her breast. His fingers didn't move, or not much, but just lay there, clamped to her breast. At least he was no longer at her ear but was once again sipping a beer, staring off into space. I looked up at the TV that was showing a section of the empty track.

'We'd pack up a blanket and dishes and plates and pack them all into a box.' I could see the box now, making it wood, an old mandarin orange crate. Was that big enough? I made it big enough, if you knew how to pack everything just right, the way we did. I imagined a river. 'And we'd drive out into the country, along an old side road, and stop by a little stream? We'd always go to the same spot, our spot by the river?' I still stared up at the TV, watching the empty track. 'And it was just the three of us, you and Mom and me? Going to our secret place on the river? Do you remember that, Dad? Do you remember that?' Because I almost could. I could almost see it, see this happy family with their picnic and their little stream flowing by. More than anything I needed that little stream to be real, to be a happy memory.

'Sure,' my dad said, though he couldn't have really heard all the crap I was making up, 'sure, by the river.'

'I'll be outside,' I said. I went out and walked through the bleachers and right down to the edge of the track. I leaned against the railing and watched the horses come out and line up and all the rest of it. I was right by the finish line and this time I noticed the jockeys whipping the horses as they thundered down to the finish. Slashing at their backs and sides with little whips, as if the horses weren't already running just as fast as they possibly could. I didn't know what to watch after that, or where to go. When the winning jockey walked away after having his picture taken, I wanted to run after him and push him down. I wanted to grab his whip and hit him with it, ask him how he felt, how he liked it now. But I didn't. I let him walk away because I knew there was nothing I could do to help the horses. And I think I was afraid that what I was feeling was stupid, little-kid worries, and that by even having those feelings I was failing at something larger, some test of adulthood. After quite a while standing there, watching a race go by, then looking out on the empty track, then watching another race, I went back to the bar.

My dad was sitting by himself, slumped in on himself in his chair. As I sat down the waiter came by and picked up the two beer, one full and one half gone, that were in front of my dad. He picked them up in one hand, a finger inside each glass pinning it to his thumb. He didn't seem to care that his fingers went into the beer, or that he spilled beer across our table. 'He's cut off,' the waiter said to me. 'Time to take Daddy home.' He laughed at that, pleased with himself. 'Time to take Daddy home.' He turned and walked back to the bar. I watched him pour the beer out and place the empty glasses upside-down in the glass washer.

I shook my father, grabbing him by his shoulder and rattling him hard. 'Come on, Dad, we have to go.' You hear people talking to drunks and they always use this particular voice. It's a voice I hate, the same voice you hear when you're a little kid and being told something completely obvious by an adult. But it's a voice that works and I used it now. 'Come on, Dad, we're going.' I stood up and tried to heave him to his feet, grabbing under his arms and pulling.

'Where's Shirley?' he said, half rising before sinking back into his chair. 'Where Shirley?' His voice was that mixture of belligerent and contrite, a drunk's voice, a voice of his I knew well. Only this time, rather than playing against my mother's quiet insistence it was playing against mine.

'She's gone, Dad. I don't know. She's gone. Come *on*, Dad, we have to go.' I got right behind him and really put my back into it. He finally realized what was happening and, together, we got him to his feet.

'Shirley's gone?' he asked me, looking around as if he might find her hiding in one of the corners.

'Yes, Dad, Shirley's gone. Jesus.'

He nodded several times as if working it all out in his mind. Then he took one of those detours that maybe you need twenty beer to follow. 'I'm no good, Gary. I'm no damn good at all. You and your mother, you and your mother –'

Jesus, he's going to start crying, I thought. 'Come on, Dad, let's go.' I put my arm around his shoulder and half carried, half dragged him out of the bar. Once up the stairs and through the doors he seemed to come around a little bit and we made it through the betting room and back outside again without a problem. Back under the concrete letters that welcomed us to Ex Park. He was moving fine, head down and walking quickly, when he stopped suddenly in the middle of the parking lot.

'Wait,' he said. 'You wait.' He lurched off between two parked cars, disappearing into the shadows. I turned away, looking to see if anyone else was in the deserted parking lot, waiting for the familiar noises to begin. After a couple of false starts, like the moans of someone in deep pain, my father was violently and noisily sick. I heard a wave of his vomit splash against the pavement, him gasp raggedly for breath, then another wave. He retched a third time, a deep writhing sound from down low, but nothing came. I heard him spit, hawk up phlegm and God knows what from the back of his throat, and spit again. Still I didn't turn around, just kept staring out at all the cars all neatly lined up in their rows.

'OK,' my father said, 'let's go.' He put his arm around my shoulder and, leaning on me, led us off to the bus-stop.

The bus shelter on Hastings was empty, since the races were still on. My father hadn't even lasted until the last race. I sat him down on the bench and, in the light from the street, saw that his shoes and pantlegs were splashed with vomit. He sat with his elbows on his knees, head hanging down, spitting dryly between his feet. The King of Siam. I searched my pockets and found change enough for both of us to get home, then went and leaned against a post, looking down the street for the bus.

We waited almost forty minutes, me against my post, my dad either spitting between his shoes or rocked back, eyes closed, half asleep against the back of the shelter. Only one person came by the whole time, an older woman with a heavy shopping bag, and she made one of those 'tchkk' noises with her teeth when she saw my dad. She was careful to give him lots of room as she passed, moving right over to the edge of the sidewalk. She shook her head at me as if to say, 'Isn't it a shame,' and I rolled my eyes at her in agreement. Like it was the two of us who were family and this guy, this drunk on the bench, was some pathetic stranger. Then she was gone and I had something else to feel lousy about.

By the time the bus came my father was out cold, his head resting on his chest. I yelled at the driver to hold on and shook the hell out of my dad. He opened his eyes, looked square at me and said, deadly serious and completely incomprehensible as only a stone drunk can be, 'One monkey doesn't make a circus, Gary. You remember that.' He closed his eyes.

'Jesus, Dad, wake up.' I was almost hysterical with frustration. I grabbed his arm and as violently as I could yanked him to his feet. Once up he stayed up, rocking back and forth, and I put his arm around my shoulder and with him leaning on me walked him to the bus.

The bus driver was watching all this through the windows of the closed door. I got Dad to the curb but the driver didn't open the door right away. He stared at us for a few more seconds and then something must have made up his mind for him because, finally, the door wheezed open. I wrestled my dad up the stairs into the empty bus.

The driver said nothing as I struggled to get my father to a seat. Once I had him propped him up, face smeared against the window, eyes closed, I returned to the driver. I counted out the change, dropping coins from my right hand into the palm of my left, eyes down, hoping that if I could just move ahead from minute to minute, eventually the night would be over.

I dropped the coins in the chute. I really looked at the driver for the first time. He was a big guy, his chest and arms tight in the blue driver's jacket. He probably thought himself tough, or near-tough, because he had one of those biker's moustaches that dropped down almost to his chin. He sat leaning forward, forearms resting on the big flat steering wheel, head turned to look at me. His eyes flicked over my father and back at me.

'Tough night,' he said, a little smile on his face.

I think now he meant it to be friendly. I think probably he looked at this sixteen-year-old kid and at his father stinking of puke and stale beer and he tried to make the kid's night maybe one percent better. Looking back I like to think that was what he was doing.

But I lost my mind. My dad, me, my mom, the crappy little picnic river that never existed, the jockeys in their crummy little boots whipping the horses, everything seemed to explode out of me at the same time.

'Fuck you!' I screamed at the bus driver. 'Fuck you, you don't know anything. You don't know anything about us!' My voice was a high screech in my ears, the voice of a child, and I didn't care. I tried to say something more to the driver, something important, something adult, but nothing could get past my shuddering sobs. Tears and snot ran down my face and I wiped them with my sleeve. I took a long jerky breath, then another. I was shaking so hard I thought I might fall down. And the driver watched all of this without doing or saying a thing, maybe afraid to interrupt me, maybe something else. I was still crying, but now I'd pulled myself back into some kind of self-control. I rubbed at my eyes again, staring hard. 'That's my dad,' I said. 'That's my dad.'

The driver shrugged, then turned and put the bus in motion. I went and sat next to my father who woke up enough to lean against me and then fall back asleep, his head on my shoulder. We stayed like that all the way home.

That's my last real memory of my father. It's something I cling to, for whatever reason.

Oh, Henry

THIS MIGHT GET A little weird,' Sharon says. 'So I want to thank you now for coming with me.' They're sitting together in the back of Sharon's mom's old car. Sharon's mom is driving and the seat beside her is filled with a huge suitcase, so Sharon and Rowena hunch together in the back like two eight-year-olds. Sharon talks in a normal voice, not at all concerned that her mother can likely hear.

'*Very* weird,' Sharon says. 'Just so you understand.' She pats Rowena on her knee, thanks, then goes back to watching her mother guide the car down the road. She does this so intently it's as if the force of her will alone keeps the car out of the ditch.

Rowena doesn't understand a thing, actually. She hardly knows Sharon, doesn't know Sharon's mother at all, isn't sure she wants to. She's known her for all of about eight minutes, the length of time they've been driving. At about minute five Sharon's mom grunted, the first noise she'd made, and said, 'Rowena, huh?'

Rowena told her, yes, Rowena, and leaned forward, ready for whatever came next.

'Huh,' Sharon's mom said. Then again, 'Huh.'

Sharon and Rowena work together at Beeker's Insurance, Rowena just for the past four months, since her divorce and everything that entailed, Sharon for ever, as far as Rowena can tell. Sharon is pretty down on Beeker's, but Rowena likes it. It's only been four months though, so you can't really tell.

One of the things she likes is what you get to find out. All those files, all those lives. One of those lives, one life in particular, was Sharon's father. Claim disallowed: suicide. So that was something else sharing the back seat with them; Sharon, Rowena, and Sharon's disallowed dad. Huh.

The car rattles along, Sharon's mom humming to herself, Sharon leaning to watch over her shoulder like a kid. Rowena beginning to wonder if maybe something is a little wrong with the whole family. Which makes her think about the disallowed dad and how he did it.

They don't put things like that in the files, though. Maybe it was in this very car, who knows? Rowena runs her fingernails over the worn red vinyl of the seat. Sharon is still staring down the road and so doesn't see when Rowena pushes one nail through, a dagger thrust in and out.

Sharon's mom turns a corner and the car feels like it's going to flip over. They can't be moving faster than twenty miles an hour, but the shocks are so bad that Rowena slides clear over next to Sharon, who doesn't seem to notice but gives Rowena a little bump with her hips, oomph, and puts her back in place. Rowena is beginning to think that Sharon's dad did the right thing.

But still. Sharon is her only friend in this town, if you want to call what they share a friendship.

'What?' says Sharon's mom.

'Nothing,' says Rowena.

'It's *always* something,' says Sharon's mom.

'Not this time.'

Maybe there's something wrong with the whole *town*. Rowena didn't exactly research the place before she moved. Just picked it more or less at random and then set out. No, that's wrong. She picked it exactly at random, like in the movies, like you're supposed to do when you start a new life. Open a map, close your eyes and drop a finger. Next time, she'll peek. These things only work out in the movies. In real life you wind up … well, you wind up exactly where she is now.

Sharon is pointing, her arm wobbling in front of Rowena's face like a plate of Spam-coloured jelly. Which is not a nice thing to be thinking and is not at all fair to Sharon. Look at her mom, for instance, and you'll know Sharon never had a chance. Rowena is, of course, ashamed of this thought. But she's also a little bit thrilled. Part of it is the flat-out pettiness of it, but another part is relief that, no matter what else goes wrong for her, she's still better off than Sharon and her Spammy arms. Pretty much, when you add everything in.

'There,' Sharon says, 'that's where we're going.' The road, which has been running more or less straight through farmers' fields and thin woods, makes a hairpin curve up ahead. On the other side of the curve, just opposite them, is where Sharon is pointing.

Rowena squints. 'A graveyard.'

'Dad,' says Sharon and nods her head. Mom doesn't say anything, just gives the old car more gas and Rowena gets ready to die half-way through the turn.

Sharon's mom parks the car on a patch of gravel that lies just through the gates. When Rowena gets out she sees there are oyster shells mixed in with the gravel. Probably the bleached white looked really nice at one time, but now not so much. It's a nice touch though, not something Rowena would have expected.

Like she wouldn't have expected Sharon's mom to become all talkative, but she has. Something about where they are, maybe, or she's warming up to the idea of Rowena coming along for the ride, who knows? But she certainly is talking.

'Three years,' she says, like this means something. Then, when nobody says anything, Rowena because she doesn't know what's going on, Sharon because she is now pointedly ignoring the whole situation, she says it again. 'Three years. To this very day.' And she smiles at Rowena and then opens the passenger door and tries to wrestle the suitcase out.

'He did it three years ago to this very day,' she says, tugging on the suitcase which has wedged itself between the seat and the dash-board. And Rowena suddenly knows what she's talking about. She panics a little when she realizes that she's going to hear all about it, there's no way around it, and looks to Sharon for help. But Sharon has walked away from the car, her steps making determined scrunch-ing noises in the gravel and shells, then no sound at all as she walks away over the matted grass that surrounds all the markers and stones.

Sharon's mom is cheerfully wrenching on the suitcase – what is *in* that thing? – not twisting it or moving it to try a different approach like you'd expect a normal person to do, but simply tugging on its handles and cramming it tighter and tighter into the bind it's in. She smiles at Rowena, stopping her efforts for a second and actually gasping for breath. 'They never found the body, you know.'

What? 'Here,' says Rowena, 'let me help you with that.' Which makes Sharon's mom beam. A very pleasant-looking woman, really, despite the family arms, probably in her early sixties with home-permed hair and a cardigan sweater over her best dress. Crazy as a loon, thinks Rowena, but pleasant-looking.

The case is heavier than it looks and bumps against Rowena's leg as they follow after Sharon. Ahead Sharon is still ignoring them, the graveyard, the birds that scream at her from the fir trees that surround the area, everything. Which doesn't seem to bother her mom, so Rowena figures it's best to let it go. Besides, by now she's burning to know what, exactly, is in this case she's carrying. Curiosity, that's a failing with her, she's been told that, she was always one to know a secret.

Which has a lot to do with what she's doing here at the graveyard. And here in this little town for the past four months. She never could let well enough alone, she always had to get to the bottom of things. Which on the one hand means humping this case over hill and dale so Sharon's mom can do who knows what at the empty grave of Sharon's disallowed dad.

And, on the other hand, it meant staking out her husband, thinking she'd catch him in bed with a seventeen-year-old named Tiffany with too much make-up and breasts up around her collar bones. But there was no Tiffany, at least none that she could discover. Not that she didn't keep trying. Or any other reason that her husband would admit to. He just left, goodbye, so long, and that was it. And how are you supposed to deal with a thing like that?

Maybe it's a trombone, or a tenor sax like she wanted to play in the high-school band until they talked her into the clarinet. Tenor saxes were supposed to be for the boys. Maybe Sharon's mom had held out against them. Maybe she is going to play some kind of soulful jazz piece for her three-years-departed husband. Rowena looks around. Theirs is the only car nosed in on the gravel and oyster shell, no one else is in sight amongst the headstones. What the hell, let 'er rip.

If that's what it is. Now she is really burning for some answers. And what did she mean they never found the body? Where was it and how did he, you know, how did he do it? Questions, questions. Curiosity can be a terrible thing, she thinks, and switches the case to her other hand. Sharon's mom has got ahead of her and Rowena has to hurry to catch up.

Sharon is waiting for them. 'Come on,' she says, gripping Rowena by the arm, the one carrying the suitcase. Rowena looks and sees that Sharon's mom has stopped and is looking down at a stone rising out of a clump of grass. That must be where he is, she thinks. She reconsiders. That must be where he would be, if he were here. Then Sharon is tugging harder on her arm and they move away. 'We'll leave her alone for a few minutes,' Sharon says. 'Besides, it gives me the creeps.'

There's a path that runs around the edge of the cemetery and they walk on that. Rowena hadn't thought to put the suitcase down, so now she has to carry it with her. It's heavy, and getting more so the more they walk. She'll have a bruise in the morning the way the thing is crashing against her leg. Sharon either doesn't notice or won't comment on the suitcase. Rowena switches it from side to side, stopping each time to do so, but Sharon just stops right along with her and doesn't say a word. It's driving Rowena nuts.

But now Sharon has decided to talk. 'It's been three years,' she says, not looking at Rowena, 'three years to the day since he did it.' Yes, yes, thinks Rowena, I *know* that.

'He took a ferry to the mainland and halfway across he jumped over the side.' Sharon doesn't look at her as she says this.

'He jumped over the side,' Rowena repeats, like an idiot, but what else is she going to say? She doesn't have a lot of experience with conversations like this. And then Sharon starts to laugh, starts to laugh really quite hard, and Rowena is a little concerned that she'll become hysterical.

But, no, Sharon is just fine. 'Actually,' she says, and now she's once more straight-faced and looking at Rowena in all seriousness, 'he hopped.' Rowena doesn't have the slightest idea what she's talking about but she'll be damned if she'll ask. She can be as stubborn as the next person, as the next *two* people, even if those two people are Sharon and her mom.

They round the last curve and head back towards Sharon's mom and the grave. It's a small graveyard. Rowena's waiting for Sharon to say more, but Sharon's in no hurry. Is it really a grave, Rowena wonders, when there's no body? They're almost there; Rowena's mom hears the sound of their feet on the gravel and looks up. She reaches for the case and Rowena, inexplicably, feels a slight pang at having to give it up.

'I hate this,' Sharon says. Her mother doesn't seem to hear. She's bent over the case, opening the big brass snaps that hold it closed.

'I really hate this part,' Sharon says again. She grabs Rowena by the arm and pulls her back, away from the grave and Sharon's mom.

'What's going on?' Rowena whispers, giving in, OK, they win. Her voice sounds like a hiss in her own ears. 'What's she doing?'

Sharon rolls her eyes. 'He went down to the car deck in the middle of the crossing and took off all his clothes.' One of the snaps is stuck, or locked, and Sharon's mom is jiggling it back and forth. If she can hear Sharon she gives no sign.

'He took off all his clothes, piece by piece, and folded them neatly and put them on the ground.'

'Someone saw him?' Rowena asks, details suddenly important.

'No, no one *saw* him,' Sharon says, rolling her eyes at Rowena now. 'They found his clothes, all in a neat little stack, everything folded – jacket, shirt, undershirt, pants, underpants, and socks – all in a neat little pile on top of his shoes.' The way she recites this list makes Rowena again wonder about the sanity of the whole family. There's something a little … obsessive about the whole crew.

Sharon's mom finally manages to open the suitcase. OK, thinks Rowena, now we'll see. I wonder what song she'll play. She considers. What if they're required to sing along?

Sharon digs her fingers into Rowena's arm. She speaks quickly, her voice insistent. Her eyes are just a little bit wild, like she is in a race to tell something to Rowena before her mom can finish whatever it is she's doing.

'He left it all stacked in a pile, neatly folded.' This is supposed to mean something, but Rowena cannot imagine what. Then, watching her mother who is still inexplicably bent over the open case, Sharon whispers: 'It must have been very cold on the deck. The wind, the steel deck under his foot as he balanced there.'

Rowena nods her head, though she has no idea what is happening here. 'He weighted it all down,' Sharon says, 'to keep the clothes from blowing away. He didn't leave a note, nothing, but he made sure that his clothes weren't swept away.' Maybe Sharon is beginning to cry, but maybe not. Rowena can't tell. This is not what she'd expected; this is nothing like anything she's done before. 'And,' says Sharon, 'he weighted it down with that.' Rowena looks and Sharon's mom has finally finished with the case. She stands and cradles in her arms an artificial leg.

Rowena feels like she's received a hammer blow to the forehead. She stares, gaping at this impossible image – Sharon's mom is now propping the leg so that it stands disembodied over the grave – and everything disappears, rushes away from her, until all that is left is an overwhelming feeling of pity and love for this woman she has known for less than an hour.

Sharon grabs her by her arm and wrenches her away. 'Come *on*,' she hisses. Then again, 'Come *on*.' She frogmarches Rowena away and they're off walking the path again, leaving Sharon's mom to whatever it is she's doing.

'It's like she thinks he'll come back or something,' Sharon says, then trudges on.

Rowena can't be sure that Sharon's not talking to herself. 'Pardon?' she says, and trots for a few feet to catch up. Sharon's walking quickly and they're already up to the first curve. Rowena wonders if this is part of the routine, if Sharon does this every year.

'She thinks he'll what?' she says, priming Sharon, caught up in all of this now, as much a part of it as either of the other two women. 'She thinks he'll come *back*?'

Sharon stops dead in her tracks and Rowena almost crashes into her, they'd been walking that fast, almost running. Sharon jerks her head back towards her mother who is, Rowena sees, simply standing there, the third in a line of objects: gravestone, leg, Sharon's mom. Rowena realizes that all this time she's been thinking of this woman as Sharon's mom. She tries to conjure a name for her, an identity that belongs to her and her only, no need for relationship, no need for anyone else. She can't do it and, besides, Sharon is talking again.

'It's like *bait*, you know? Like once a year she figures she has a chance to get him back, that if she just waits long enough, he'll return to get his….' She trails off, and Rowena isn't exactly sure why. Maybe she can't bring herself to say the word 'leg'. Maybe she's all upset again, Rowena can't say. Sharon grabs her by the arm again,

Sharon is certainly fond of arm grabbing, that's one thing she *can* do, and jerks Rowena off the path. They're at the opposite end of the graveyard from Sharon's mom, the woman with no name, though it's such a tiny place that Rowena figures she could toss a pebble and hit her. Maybe toss a larger rock and knock over the leg. Win a prize. She shakes her head to stop these kinds of thoughts. She has the vague sense that she's with the wrong person, that alliances have been drawn up and she's on the wrong side.

Sharon sits down on the grass, her back against a headstone. Rowena has no choice, she sits down too, though she's careful not to sit on top of anybody. It's not that she's superstitious, or even religious, it's just a matter of good manners. The same reason she got caught up in all this insanity in the first place.

Sharon lights a cigarette and jams the smouldering match into the grass beside her. Great, thinks Rowena, and where is she going to put the butt when she's done? Now she has something else to worry about, something else that is none of her business.

'You were married, right?' Sharon says. Rowena notices that she's careful not to blow smoke at her, so that's something, anyway.

'Right,' Rowena says. 'I was married.' She looks around, as if they're at some scenic vista somewhere. Trees, gravestones, some dirty oyster shells. She doesn't look to see what Sharon's mom is doing.

'And?'

'And I don't want to talk about it.'

Sharon puffs on her cigarette, thinking about this. Then she flicks the ember off the butt and wraps what's left in a Kleenex. Rowena watches her tuck the Kleenex into her pocket, slightly surprised, but Sharon doesn't notice.

'I'd like to have an ex-husband,' she says, leaning back against the headstone.

'*What?*' Rowena quacks, surprised yet again.

'I think it would be nice to have an ex-husband, a past that's nicely wrapped up and cut off. Something you can hand people in a neat little package. I think you're actually lucky, when you think about it.'

This is the first time that Rowena has been told she's lucky, and she does have to think about it. She's never felt sorry for herself but she hasn't exactly been overjoyed, either. One thing, she'll be lucky if she gets out of here pretty soon. She's done her bit for friendship, even one as brief and as thin as the one she and Sharon have, and now she'd just like to go.

But Sharon isn't done with it. 'Because that's more than I have,' she says, 'something that I can hand out to explain who I am and where I'm at.' She gets to her feet, pulling herself up by leaning on the headstone. Rowena stays seated, looking up at her. 'And it's certainly more than my mom has, if you want to look at it like that. All she has left is –' and she jerks her head towards her mother and the leg. Rowena doesn't bother to look; it's as if the leg has begun to fill the whole clearing and everything in it. Even with her eyes closed, she thinks, all she'll be able to see is the leg. 'That's not something you can give to people,' Sharon says, 'it's worse than nothing at all.' And then she turns and starts walking again, crunching along the oyster path.

Rowena gets up herself and walks back to the grave. Sharon's mom smiles at her, then goes back to staring at the leg and, just behind it, the grey stone marker. Rowena sees that Sharon's father was named Lloyd, and that he was born in 1932. Nothing on the stone says anything about when or how he died.

She looks at the leg. It's one of those objects that looks familiar, even if you've never seen one before. There is no possibility of it being anything other than what it is.

Sharon's mom has propped it against the headstone. If Sharon's dad were sitting on top of the stone, facing them, the leg would be in just that position. Its thigh at an angle to the stone, the leg sloping to the knee, and the knee bent so that the lower leg and foot meet the ground at close to a right angle. Rowena can practically see Sharon's ghost dad, perched there, casual, connected to the ground by that one leg.

The leg is shoeless, and she wonders about that. Maybe, she thinks, Sharon's mom wants it left just the way it was … at the end. The foot has no toes, she notices.

Sharon's mom coughs. Rowena is standing right beside her, shoulders almost touching, so when she coughs again they bump together, once, twice, like dolls on the same string. Neither of them moves, but Sharon's mom begins to speak.

'I have this dream,' she says, but that's all she says, like Rowena is supposed to know what she means. Rowena keeps staring at the stone and at the leg, at *Lloyd's* leg. She knows the name of Sharon's disallowed ghost dad, but the woman next to her, the woman close enough to bump into her when she coughs, is only Sharon's mom.

'I have this dream,' she says again, after a bit, and of course Rowena knows what's coming, more or less. 'Where he's swimming, swimming away. And he has two legs. He's a good swimmer, a strong swimmer, and he has two legs.'

'Jesus!' says Sharon, she's come up on them somehow without Rowena noticing. 'Jesus, Mom! Is this all really necessary?' And then she's stomping off, kicking pieces of oyster shell out of her way, marching to the other end of the cemetery again. Rowena watches her go, not sure what she should do here. There's a certain ritual at work, she's pretty sure, but she has no idea what her role is.

Sharon's mom rustles in her purse. Rowena is watching her now, staring at her in a way that would seem rude in other circumstances. Here, suddenly, rules like that no longer apply.

She pulls out not a Kleenex like you'd expect, but a chocolate bar, an Oh Henry! in its bright yellow wrapper. She holds it in two hands and then snaps it in half, still in its wrapper. She hands half to Rowena. 'Oh He' the piece says, and Rowena does her best not to see any significance in this.

'Thank you,' says Rowena.

'You're welcome,' says Sharon's mom. And then they both turn back to stare again at the leg, chewing together in silence.

Sharon is still off at the far end of the cemetery, furiously smoking another cigarette. She tosses her head, flicking it from side to side, making a large point of not looking in their direction. Rowena has no idea what is making her so angry, but she figures that it's her business and no one else's. She's starting to think that Sharon doesn't really need a reason, or not a very big one, anyway.

Rowena mulls this over as she finishes her chocolate bar, which is very good. She licks her fingers and then hands the empty wrapper to Sharon's mom, who has held her hand out for it. Sharon's mom crumples the two half-wrappers up into a ball and tucks it back in her purse. All the while they've been staring at the leg, at the stone, in the ghostly direction of Lloyd, gone but definitely not forgotten.

Sharon's mom turns now and stares off in the other direction. Rowena turns too and sees that from where they're standing there really is a view. Through the trees there is a clear patch of sky and outlined against that, far in the distance, is a mountain range and the white smudge of a glacier. 'That's beautiful,' Rowena says.

'Sharon tells me you were married,' Sharon's mom says.

'Yes, I was,' Rowena says.

'What happened?'

Jesus, what *happened*? An earthquake happened, a tidal wave, locusts and poisonous toads fell from the sky. 'I don't know,' Rowena says. 'He left. It was over, I guess.' She thinks about it, as if she hadn't considered it before. For some reason she wants to do right by this woman. 'I don't know.'

Sharon's mom nods, still staring at the glacier, not looking at Rowena. Rowena looks at her, though, and thinks for the second time that this is a nice-looking woman, a friendly, nice woman.

'Why do you do this?' Rowena asks.

'This?'

'Come here, bring the leg, all of it. Sharon thinks that you believe he'll come back. That somehow he'll return to get his leg. Is that what you believe?'

Sharon's mom is perfectly still. She doesn't say anything for a second and then, 'No,' she says, 'I don't believe that.'

Rowena can't leave it alone. 'Then why? Why do you do it?'

Sharon's mom turns now and looks at her. 'Because it helps,' she says.

Sharon is waiting for them. They pack up the leg, load the car, and are off in less than two minutes. Driving away, Rowena hopes that she gets to do this again next year. She'd like that, she thinks, that is something she'd really like to do.

The Promised Land

MOOKEY LIVINGSTON, IN THE short space of just under one week, lost his piece-of-crap, sometimes-yes, sometimes-no job; got thrown out of her apartment by a woman who said if she saw him again she'd have him beaten up, or arrested, or both; *and* beat the shit out of four separate home games. These were serious games, mind, run twenty-four hours a day in apartments with four and five locks on the door. Serious games and very serious players. Added up, he walked with over thirty-eight hundred dollars, the most money by a long shot that he'd ever won.

With the thirty-eight folded in, his bankroll totalled out at just over seventy-two hundred dollars, cash. He thought it over for about two seconds, staring down at the stacks of beautiful worn bills, then booked the first flight for Vegas. Walking through the metal-detector doohickey at the airport he said out loud to himself: you've got to play your rush, there's just nothing else you can do.

Las Vegas. He'd never even set eyes on the place but it felt like he'd been missing it his whole life. He was the best poker player he knew. The local fools and dim-bulb hard guys had to know it too as they handed over their losings every week but still he couldn't get respect. Vegas would be different for him. Everything would work out just fine.

Which kept him in a good mood, big smile on his face, the whole trip. Even when, an hour into the flight, this big guy in a tie and one of those short-sleeve dress shirts, maybe the captain, who knows, told him that he was cut off from any more alcoholic beverages and that if he tried to touch the hostess again he'd be taken off the plane in handcuffs when they landed. Even with this big joker scowling down at him Mookey couldn't stop smiling. Fuck 'em, they had no idea who they were dealing with.

But the guy sitting next to him turned out to be OK. He watched the captain strut back up the aisle, then passed a full can of beer to Mook. Which, to tell the truth, he really didn't need since he'd been hitting it pretty hard, but it just went to show what kind of a roll he was on. He toasted the guy and pecked at the fresh can. Playing his rush.

The guy was travelling with about six others, all in matching leather ball caps. They worked as loggers 'in camp', whatever that meant. 'We're down for five days and four nights and we're not stopping,' the guy told him. His name was Buck. Buck was maybe twenty years old, weighed about a hundred and twenty-eight pounds, and the stewardess looked more like a logger than he did. 'Gonna play us some blackjack, gonna play us some craps, gonna party for five days and four nights. How about you, partner?'

Mookey sipped at his beer and tried to look bored. 'Poker,' he said. 'I'm a professional. And –' the thought came to him as he said the words, '– and I'm not coming back.' Which impressed Buck no end. Impressed Mookey too, come to that. He looked out the window, down at the rolling brown hills of the desert, and wondered what he was getting himself into. He raised his beer. 'Cheers,' he said.

He ditched the leather-heads in the airport, left them milling around the luggage carousel and didn't look back. Walking away not just from them but from everyone like them, past and future. He was a pro now.

He jumped in the first taxi he saw and told the cabbie to take him where they played poker. 'Serious poker?' the cabbie asked. Mookey nodded, sure, what other kind was there. 'You'll want the Shoe, Binion's Horseshoe.'

The cab was already moving, though so far the road looked like nothing special, not yet. More like the driveway to a second-rate strip-mall which, come to think, is what the airport looked like. Mook settled back, watching the road, careful not to think too much about what he was doing or how he was going to do it. 'Right. Take me there. Take me to the Shoe.'

The driver took him downtown by way of the Strip. He told him it was to show him what they'd done to Vegas, 'Turned it into a fucking amusement park. Giant lions, pyramids. People bringing their fucking kids with them.' He shook his head, mourning Vegas's loss, and told Mook how smart he was to be staying downtown, in the real Vegas, the old town.

He was right about the pyramid, and the lion too. Mook saw what looked like Cinderella's castle but didn't ask about it. 'Like a fucking amusement park,' he told the cabbie.

'A fucking amusement park,' the cabbie agreed. 'Told you.'

Downtown on the other hand was almost quaint. Smaller, with buildings that except for their huge neon signs looked like nothing other than buildings. Binion's was on the corner, wrapped around the corner, what could have been a furniture store or family restaurant but topped by a three-story bank of turquoise neon lights. 'Binion's Horseshoe Club' the signs said. Mook paid off the cabby, took a breath, and walked in.

The noise completely overwhelmed him. Bells ringing, sirens going off. People yelling, hollering things he couldn't make out over the roar. It was hell on earth, people crammed in practically shoulder to shoulder, wedged into a room made tiny by their numbers. The flashing red lights from the tops of the slot-machines made it like walking in in the middle of some kind of fire alarm.

Except people kept coming, more and more of them. He didn't see any poker, just row after row of slot machines with people parked on little stools in front of them. And over it all, a wall of noise like nothing he'd heard.

He looked around, maybe he was in the wrong place, maybe the cabbie had ripped him off, and a huge guy in some kind of guard's uniform tapped him on the shoulder. 'Can I help you, sir?' the guy, kid really, maybe only twenty-five or so, asked. He was wearing the biggest handgun Mookey had ever seen and for a second he wondered if now he was in for real trouble.

But it turned out the kid just wanted to help. He directed Mook to the check-in desk and then, when Mookey had walked in a circle – the room was bigger than he'd thought, a series of small room joined end to end, like a maze once you crammed it with thousands of people and machines and, now that he looked, kidney shaped blackjack tables – he picked up Mookey's bag and walked it and him to the desk. By this time Mookey was starting to settle in and was quick enough to have a dollar bill ready for him when they arrived. 'That's not necessary, sir,' the kid said. He didn't look all that impressed but he took it anyway. Maybe it should have been a five. But when he tried to give the clerk at the desk a five she wouldn't take it at all. Mook would take a while to figure things out. Which was OK, he had the time.

When he told the girl, the one who wouldn't take the five, that he planned on staying, he didn't know exactly how long but he was here to play some poker, she stopped what she was doing. 'Oh,' she said, 'then you'll want our poker rate.' Which turned out to be a special deal, just for poker players. Just for people like him. And, she explained, there was a whole system of 'comps', which meant even better deals, free food and beverages, maybe even a free room. Comps. She arranged to have his bag taken right up to his room by an honest-to-god bellboy in a little red suit, only the cap missing, who *would* take Mookey's five dollars, so that Mookey could go directly to the poker room. 'Ask for George at the desk,' she said, 'and we'll fix you right up. You enjoy your stay now, Mr. Livingston.'

'Aw, honey,' he said, 'you can call me Mookey.'

He got directions to the poker room, twice, then figured he'd have a drink first, get the lay of the land. You couldn't walk more than about ten feet without crossing another little bar, six or ten stools lined up along a counter, guy in a black bow tie pouring drinks.

He pulled up a stool and nodded at the guy in the bow tie. 'The name's Mookey. Gimme a beer.' What the hell, 'Have one for yourself.'

The bartender nodded. 'Appreciate it, Mookey. Where you from?' He gave Mookey a bottle of Bud and a glass but took nothing for himself. He waved off the five that Mookey held out. 'Welcome to Binion's.'

Mook squinted to read the bartender's name-tag. 'As of right now, Stan, I'm from here,' he said. 'I'm from right here.'

Only two others were seated at the bar, sitting together a couple of stools down. On the far side a craggy old guy in some kind of velour track outfit was hunkered down over his drink, staring into the glass. 'I'm drinking myself sober,' he said, more to his drink than to the guy next to him. 'You drink to a certain point, you're drunk. What you got to do is move through that, move past it. Drink yourself sober. After that, you'll be all right.'

The man on the next stool, closer to Mookey, easily young enough to be the first guy's son, snorted. 'That's just about the dumbest damn thing I've heard anyone say. Today anyway.' He looked at his watch, a clunky gold affair with what looked like nuggets welded to its body. 'Course, it's not yet noon. Still, that's an awful goddamn stupid thing to say.'

The older man ignored him. He took a showy last swig of his drink and signalled Stan for another. 'You got to drink yourself sober, that's the thing. Then you'll be ready to play.' He stayed slouched over his drink but swivelled his head to peer down the bar at Mookey, stare for a second, then turn back to his glass.

Mook finished half his beer before anyone spoke. Then the old guy started in all over again, speaking with the perfect, clear pronunciation of someone trying hard to communicate from behind a thick fog of alcohol. 'In big game fishing, when they go after the marlin and the big sharks, they draw action with chum. Blood and guts and ground body parts. Toss it overboard by the bucketful to stir them up, keep 'em interested. And to these guys –' and here he jerked his head at something Mookey couldn't see, ' – we're chum. That's all there is to it. Something ground up and tossed over the side.'

The young guy snorted again, then looked up and rolled his eyes at Mookey. 'Breakfast of champions,' he said, and raised his beer bottle in salute.

Mookey nodded at him, put his Bud down and stood up. Maybe he'd wait. He tucked the five under his beer and walked away. These guys are lepers, he told himself. These are not people you want to be around.

The bartender called after him. 'Thanks, Mook, see you next time.' So he was getting the hang of this after all.

Or not. George turned out to be a young woman standing behind a desk at the entrance to a roped-off area. The poker room. Maybe twenty oval tables, nowhere near as many as he'd expected. About two-thirds of them in use, each one crowded with nine or ten people. Men mostly, but a few women. Mostly old guys though, lots of sweat suits, rumpled clothes. One really old guy whizzed past Mookey as he stood there, driving one of those electric wheel-

chair/golf-cart things. He had a captain's hat on his head and had to
be ninety. Watching him back that cart into place at a table, swivel
the seat and commence playing, Mook had a sudden vision of the
same guy sixty years ago. A young man, snappy dresser, strutting to
the card table.

It seemed like everyone wore heavy gold jewellery. Thin,
expensive watches, huge rings, clunky bracelets and necklaces, even
on the men. Mookey looked at his bare hands, his cheap little electric
watch, and already felt like something was missing.

'Sir? Sir, would you like to play some poker? Sir?' George was
waiting for him to finish with his gawking. She smiled patiently, like
she went through this a lot. Her name-tag told him her name,
George, and that she was from Billings, Montana.

'Sure,' Mook said. He took a breath. 'Sign me up.'

'What would you like? I've got openings at pot-limit hold'em and
20-40 Omaha. We're running a list for 5-10 and 10-20 hold'em. And
we've got a list for seven stud, but it's a real long one.'

Mookey blinked, then looked over the sea of tables and players.
Except for seven-card stud, he had no idea what George had just
said. And his impulse, a strong one, was to get far away from there as
fast as he could.

'Um, 5-10?' he asked, making it a question, hoping he didn't
sound too stupid. Maybe this all wasn't such a good idea after all.

She nodded. 'We play mostly structured limit here, sir. The bet
doubles to ten dollars on the turn and the river.'

He closed his eyes and rubbed them. 'River?' No possible chance
now of keeping his dignity.

'Oh,' she said, 'you haven't played poker before.' You could actually see her change gears as he diminished in front of her. 'OK,
hold'em is a simple game. Everyone gets two cards and then the betting opens after the big and little blinds have been put in.'

'I'll be right back,' he told her. And fled.

But when the double doors locked behind him he saw that he'd
made another mistake. A fire exit, or something like it, had emptied
him into an alley. Nothing but clumps of litter and a dented and rust-
ing Dumpster. The silence a physical shock after the roar of the
casino. Right, he thought, great, and headed for the street.

He was just alongside the Dumpster when a pile of garbage moved, transformed into the homeless person who had been curled up there. 'Hey, tourist,' the man hissed at him, 'spare some change?'

He shook his head, no, and moved past. But the man reached out and grabbed Mook's ankle, pinching it tightly in his hand. Mook looked down, shocked, and saw the dirty, hairy face grinning at him. Then he saw the tiny pistol, pointed right at his own face.

In some kind of reflex he tried to jerk his leg away but the man jumped to his feet, still pointing the gun. He slapped Mook across the face, hard. The gun didn't waver. 'I said, "Hey, tourist, you got any spare change?"'

He emptied Mook's wallet, then tossed it down the alley. 'Lie down.' Mook didn't move. 'You lie down now.'

'Please,' Mook said. 'Please don't.'

'You lie down,' the man said again. 'If you get up, if you even look up, I'll shoot you dead.'

Mook got down on his knees, then collapsed flat on the grimy concrete, his face pressed hard against a ground-down cigarette butt, who knew what else. 'Please,' he whispered again. 'Please.' He started to cry.

'Hey, tourist?' The man's face was directly above his own. 'Hey, tourist? Welcome to Las Vegas.' The laughter and the footsteps carried down the alley as the man ran away.

2.

'AND THAT ACTUALLY HAPPENED?'

Mook sipped his bottle of water and shrugged, like it was all nothing. 'My first day. Practically my first hour. Welcome to Las Vegas.'

His companion, Dick or Rick, something like that, whistled softly. 'They should put that one in the flyers, maybe a billboard. "Visit Downtown and Die".' He whistled again. 'Boy, oh boy.'

Mook nodded, already bored with the story he'd been telling for six months. But, in a town built on the promise of glamour and riches, the next best thing is a true story of humiliation and terror. Everyone has to be someone, even if that someone is a loser and victim. Besides, it gave him a chance to show how far he'd come. What a dumb fuck: first all that drunk asshole crap on the plane. Then the kicker: walking into Binion's like he knew what he was doing. Laying himself open by walking down an alley, down an *alley* for Christ's sake, in downtown. At this point he usually took a sip of water, considered for a few seconds, then delivered the punch line.

But Dick beat him to it. 'It could have been worse, you could have actually played *poker* against those guys in there.' And he laughed at that, because it was true and they both had to know it.

Mookey just toyed with his bracelet and wondered how many times he'd told that story. Maybe one time too many. He poured the last ounce of water out into his hand and rubbed his face and back of his neck. 'Back to work,' he said and stood up.

Rick or Dick, whatever the hell his name was, just grunted. He'd been running very bad for almost three weeks and was stuck at least eight thousand that Mookey knew of. Which might not be much to the boys who played at the big tables at Binion's or the Mirage, but for small-timers like them, well, Mookey knew just what it meant. He walked away and didn't look back. If he had to bet, he'd lay odds that Dick would trade his bottle of Mountain Valley water for shots of bourbon any time now. And that whatever was left of Dick's bankroll would soon follow the eight. He thought of what he'd heard his first hour in town. Chum, that's what Dick was, blood and body parts to be thrown over the side.

On that first day at least he'd been smart enough to keep most of his money in his sock, tucked in tight under his instep. So the guy got away with maybe four hundred, and most of Mook's self-respect back when he had some, but it wasn't the end of the world. More like the beginning of it, if you wanted to think of it that way. A harsh lesson but one Mookey took to heart. And that, he was convinced, is how you made it in this town: you learned from your losses. Anyone can be a winner, for a time, but if you can turn your failures around, save them up, use them, well, that was what it took.

So now he played in the tourist games, 4-8, 5-10, trying to scratch enough together to move up. Treating it seriously, like a job, like what it was – factory work. In the meantime he worked the graveyard shift, midnight to seven, tending bar at the Oasis. Serving Bud after Bud, Jim Beam on the side, giving advice on how to beat the slots, what the best system for blackjack was, whatever the tourists wanted to hear. Ask them their names, where they're from, say: See that guy over there, he's connected, a made man. Kansas City mob. 'Really?' the tourists would say, accountants on a tear, farmers, bankers, whatever, looking for a little of the danger and glamour they'd heard about. Peeking at the guy Mook had just pointed out, usually his shift boss, Terry, who collected little porcelain dolls as a hobby and couldn't find Kansas City with a map. Saving every detail to tell the folks back home. Absolutely, he'd say. Absolutely, but let's just keep that between you and me. They practically threw the tips at him, they were so happy.

Each stool was parked in front of a video poker terminal. So, as long as the tourists played, the drinks were free. The fun part was letting them think they were getting away with something. Give 'em a roll of quarters and a Bud for ten dollars, then watch them blink as they figured it out. Act like little kids, stashing the quarters away, then offering him another ten for a roll and a Bud, hardly believing their good fortune. So, what you gave them wasn't really the drink, it was the thrill of getting away with it. A gift, a little something just for them.

He'd get off work at seven, have a double Jimbo as a nightcap and head home. The street crawling with tourists giddy from staying up all night, set to do it straight through another day. You didn't even notice them after a while, the college kids in bunches of five and six, the retired couples carrying their tubs of nickels from one slot joint to another. The first time he walked past the Promised Land slot club, all done up with clouds and harps, he laughed out loud. Now it was what it was, nothing more, nothing less.

He rented a bachelor apartment six blocks from downtown. Six blocks the wrong side of downtown, which kept the rent just manageable. He was home in ten minutes, asleep in half an hour if he was lucky. Sleep for six or seven, get six or seven hours of cards in, then work again. The promised land.

'Bump it eight.' The tourist to Mook's right splashed the pot, then swivelled his head to stare off at something in the corner of the room. Which was a tell, of course, the tourist had himself a hand, but so what? With players this bad you were wasting your time playing real poker, they weren't smart enough to know when to do the right thing. And a real hand to them could be any pair with any kind of shitty kicker. Mook tossed in another eight chips, casting them with a sideways flick of the wrist so they lay out on the table in two rows of four. Like anyone else in Vegas who played poker he could practically make the chips sit up and bark.

The last card to fall gave the tourist three fours, he'd been playing a four and a nine. Mook threw away his ace queen, he'd had top two pair the whole way, and sighed. 'Nice hand, sir,' he told the tourist.

'Damn straight,' the tourist crowed. 'You boys never had a chance.'

Mook's problem, or one of them, was that he was just a little bit happy for the guy. With any kind of luck the tourist would walk with a couple of hundred and go back a hero to wherever the hell he came from. Tell all his drinking and once-a-week home game buddies how he kicked ass in Las Vegas. Which was a little bit of a good thing for him and a very big bad thing for Mook to be thinking.

The guys at the big tables, the guys who could really play, didn't think that way. But Mook couldn't afford to move up and, he was starting to think, just maybe he lacked the heart for it. He lacked the heart for something, that was for sure. He was too good for these little-league games and not good enough or rich enough for the big ones. It was a problem. He watched the tourist order another double Chivas and tip the girl five dollars. Mook sipped at his Mountain Valley and shook his head.

He used to drink at games but that was back at the home games, back at his old life. Before he'd even heard the word hold'em, let alone played. Two or three octagonal tables set up in an apartment, bottles of rye and Scotch, a tub of beer at a buck a pop. Guys playing cards and laying down sports bets over cell phones at the same time. Playing seven stud and goofy games like high Chicago, baseball, crap like that. Games Mook could beat regularly just by staying awake. It seemed like not just a lifetime ago but someone else's lifetime. He shook his head and told himself to concentrate, act like a pro. The tourist won another pot.

He got home at eleven-thirty, just enough time to change, splash his face and head off to work. He was stuck a hundred and thirty-four dollars, which he noted carefully in his ledger. Part of being a pro was treating it like a business, making sure to add up not just your wins but your losses as well. So he'd played poker for seven and a half hours and lost one hundred and thirty-four dollars doing it. Sometimes he wondered.

At work Terry asked him, straight out, if he liked his job, if he liked being where he was. What could he say? Sure, you bet. You bet, Terry.

'OK, then.' Terry nodded, his big square head jerking up and down. He turned to go, then stopped, almost an afterthought. 'I don't want to hear any more of this Kansas City mob bullshit, you understand me, Mook? Don't fuck around with shit like that.' Mook nodded. 'You *understand* me, Mook?'

Jesus. He wanted Mook to say the words. Welcome to kindergarten. 'Sure, Terry. I understand.'

'All right.'

Which left him with not much more than 'What'll it be?' and 'Where you from?' And how do you fill seven hours a night with that and stay sane?

He stayed in a shitty mood all shift. And the shitty mood would have lasted all the way home except he was brought up short, like he was sandbagged, right outside the Promised Land. He stared, then looked around to see if maybe this was a gag, then burst out laughing. Because standing outside the Promised Land, at quarter to eight in the morning, was an honest-to-God angel.

A pretty frowzy angel, sure. An angel whose wings were likely remaindered from a show at Circus Circus or somewhere, and whose halo was spray-painted more orange than gold, but an angel nonetheless. She held a small wicker basket with a neat sign, 'Professional slot-player's gloves: FREE.' An attractive but not showy woman in her mid or late thirties, watching him watch her.

'Something amuses you, sport?'

He shook his head. 'Absolutely not. Should it?'

She looked him square in the face, giving nothing away. In a town where every woman, *every* woman was some shade of chemical blond, she had reddish-brown hair. 'That depends on whether you view life as comedy or tragedy, I guess. Where do you fall on that question?'

He surprised himself by taking the question seriously. For the first time in six months he was being asked something that had nothing to do with cards, with money, with somehow getting the best of it. He thought hard for a few seconds, wanting to do right by this woman. 'It's a strange mixture of both, don't you think? That's what makes it interesting.'

She smiled. 'You win a prize.' She held out her basket.

He took one of the ridiculous gloves, tissue-thin cotton things likely worth two cents apiece. He put it on, taking slow care to draw the fingers tight. 'Will you have dinner with me?' he asked.

'Absolutely,' she said.

Her name was Annie and she told Mookey ('Mookey?' 'Edward.' 'Right. Edward.') that she wanted to go to a restaurant that had nothing to do with a casino. And not to a buffet.

Which took some effort. When Mook woke up at two-thirty, still wearing his glove, he realized that he hadn't paid for a meal in almost six months. Hadn't eaten anywhere other than a casino coffee-shop or buffet. Had no idea if there *was* such a thing as a restaurant not connected with some kind of gambling.

He'd told her he'd pick her up at seven, which gave him some time. Gave him a lot of time, actually, since he wouldn't be able to play poker, another first. He decided to use the freedom and grabbed the black garbage bag stuffed with his laundry. He kept it in his hall closet, as far from his bed as he could. Even carefully sealed it reeked of stale cigarette smoke. Mook no longer considered it odd that he had to double-bag his laundry just to keep it in the same apartment. An occupational hazard. Didn't everyone live this way?

At least one other person did. In the laundry room another low stakes player, named Ice Cream Dave for no reason Mook could figure, was doing his chores as well. He grunted at Mook, who grunted back. 'How you running this week?' Mook asked.

'Up and down, up and down,' Ice Cream said. 'Maybe I'm even. You?'

'Same.' They both set to work on their machines. Mook knew that, whether Ice Cream had won a blue million or was stuck for his whole roll, the answer would always be 'just about even'. As was his. No poker player ever told the truth about money and no poker player ever failed to ask. Certain rituals were required.

Mook crammed his stinking clothes into the machine and punched in three quarters. Ice Cream was already done and leaning against a wall with an old issue of 'Card Player' that he had to have read thirty times already. Somehow, seeing the cover of the magazine, seeing Ice Cream, smelling the stale tobacco reek of the poker room here, out of place in what could pass for the real world, made it all seem strange. It lasted for only a moment, and Mook couldn't really put a word or a name to how it felt, but for a second the world flipped around on itself and on him. He closed his eyes, opened them, and it flipped back. Maybe not to normal, whatever that was, but at least to the thing he was accustomed to.

He waited till Ice Cream looked up. 'Say, Cream,' he said, 'I got a question for you.'

'Yeah?' Ice Cream's eyes were blank, his face uncommitted. Waiting for some kind of proposition, some percentage play from Mook, waiting to see what it was, evaluate it, accept it or counter. Poker without cards.

All of which Mook knew, and he also knew what the reaction to what he was really going to say would be, but he pressed on. 'You know a nice place to eat, like a restaurant? Some place not a buffet or in a casino, a nice restaurant?'

Ice Cream's lizard eyes flicked over Mook like he was a piece of fresh dog turd stuck to one of Cream's newly clean shirts. 'The fuck you talking about?' he said and went back to his magazine.

'I'm surprised, Edward. I didn't think you'd find a place like this.' The waiter held Annie's chair as she sat down, giving Mook a little time to look around. He was pretty impressed too. A nice Italian restaurant, linen table cloths and napkins, elegant waiters who looked like they weren't killing time waiting to get into dealer's school. Everything more or less the way it had been described over the phone. Mook had spent the better part of an hour phoning around, flipping back and forth through the yellow pages, searching for something, anything that would fill the bill. When the guy on the phone, speaking in a slow and measured Italian accent, told him that a jacket and tie were required, he knew he'd found his spot. He had to buy the tie.

He listened to the sound of Annie's voice. Sometimes you're wrong when you hear a voice and try to figure out who the person is, what they're like, but sometimes you're not. He smiled, thinking of her standing in front of the Promised Land. The voice of an angel.

'Edward?'

'I'm sorry. I was just thinking of you, in your get-up. Your wings and all. Not something you see every day.'

She smiled too. 'You have to lead the right life if you want to see angels. That's not easy to do every day.'

She was practically grinning now, so he could see it was going to be all right. He busied himself ordering a bottle of red wine from the waiter who was suddenly there, then sat back in his chair, hands flat on the tablecloth, studying Annie. Someone, he couldn't remember who, had told him that in poker, amateurs play with cards. Better players use cards and money. The pros, the thing they really knew about, the thing that mattered maybe the most in the long run, was people.

'How long have you lived here?' he asked.

'You mean, what's a nice girl like me doing in a town like this?' He still couldn't put a finger on just which side of mocking she landed. The waiter arrived with the bottle of wine and having to sort through all the nonsense with the label and the cork and the little sip and the 'Yes, that's fine, thank you' saved him from having to answer right away.

'I'm second-generation Las Vegas,' Annie said. 'I was *born* here, can you believe that? I grew up, got married, thought I'd wind up in a little house, little yard, two or three third-generation Las Vegans. The Las Vegas, Nevada, version of the American dream.' She picked up her wine glass, set it back down. 'That all went south and I left. Now I'm back. I wear feathers and a beat-up halo and everybody takes my picture. That's all there is. Your turn.'

Mook sincerely doubted that that was all there was, but he let it go. He sipped from his wine, which was expensive and very good. For some reason he admired the restaurant for having the balls to charge the moon in a town where they threw free alcohol at you by the bucketful. He watched Annie sip from her glass, replace it just so on the table, dab at her lips with her napkin, all the time watching him.

He thought about exaggerating his situation a little, build it up just a little. But something about Annie told him that she'd know, that she'd be able to read him. 'I've been here six months. I live in a little apartment just off Roberds Street and work night bar at the Oasis. After work I walk home past your place. That's how I saw you.'

'And?'

Her question threw him a little. Not because he didn't know what she was asking but because he was pretty sure he did. 'How do you know there's an "and"?'

She shook her head and half smiled, as if he had disappointed her, if only slightly. 'There's always an "and." She brushed a strand of hair from her face and looked intently at him. 'You moved here six months ago. You live in a lousy part of town and sling drinks at the Oasis, which – you remember that I grew up here – is about one step up from a Hotel 6. And....' She studied him for a few seconds. 'You don't look like a card counter to me. It's not blackjack.'

'No?'

'No. The tedium eats away at you. Pro blackjack players, counters, go dead from the eyes down. You don't look like that. You're not a counter.'

Now Mook smiled, beginning to enjoy this game. 'No, I'm not a counter.'

'And you're not a sports bettor.'

'How do you know that?'

'I just do.' She paused, more for the effect than because she was thinking, Mook was pretty sure. Then her face went very still, controlled. 'God help you, you're a poker player, aren't you?'

Mook tried to keep from grinning, but couldn't manage to keep his face flat. 'Well, I –'

'I'm sorry,' Annie said, 'I don't think this is going to work out.'

She was silent for a few seconds, visibly struggling to find words. A look of genuine grief flashed across her face and she pushed back her chair. 'I'm sorry, Edward,' she said, stood up, and was gone. Just in time for their waiter to arrive, carrying leather menus the size of screen doors. He cocked one eyebrow at Mookey, shrugged, and snapped his finger for the bill. Mook sat for a second, running it over in his mind like a play gone wrong, then reached for his wallet. He smiled at the waiter and shrugged his shoulders, but this time the elegant Italian just stared down at him.

When he got home he had three quick shots of Jimbo, then phoned the Oasis and blew off work. He hit the poker room by nine o'clock and played until ten in the morning, better than thirteen hours straight without a break. He made six dollars.

And then he had the problem of how to get home without passing the Promised Land. He was set to take a cab, he even flagged one down, then thought, fuck it. If you can't face losing, you shouldn't ever win, they went together, they had to. And the man who didn't realize that wasn't much. Still, after he waved the cab away he wasn't too thrilled with what he had to do.

Annie didn't look surprised to see him. What she did look was sad, which was not the emotion Mook was looking for. A sad angel, with her beat-up halo and scruffy wings, her little basket of two-cent cotton gloves. He just stood there, watching her watch him, maybe ten feet away. They were under the overhang of the arcade, with the neon sign that spelled out Promised Land and all the rest of that nonsense buzzing and crackling over their heads. The morning was still cool and the fresh air, the night without sleep, the thirteen hours of wasted time spent hunched over a poker table made Mook feel light-headed.

'Edward,' Annie said. 'Edward, I –

'Mookey, my name is Mookey.' He realized that his voice sounded harsh, and was a little bit glad.

Annie nodded, that sad look still on her face. 'Mookey, I'm sorry about last night. It wasn't a nice thing to do, but you have to understand that –'

'You owe me,' Mookey said. He knew enough that if she got to

say what she was going to say, he'd have been kissed-off for good, no
going back. And he also knew that he had the lead here, not a very
big one and not a very good one, but still the lead. 'You owe me,' he
said again. 'Come for lunch. One lunch. You think you know me and
maybe you do, but I deserve more from you.'

Annie shook her head but she might as well have nodded, yes,
because Mook knew that he'd made his point and that she'd agree.
'We all deserve more, Mookey, don't you think?' And then she did
say yes, just as he knew she would, he'd read her right after all.

He had her meet him at Binion's Coffee Shop. The hell with it, he
was a poker player living in Las Vegas and there was no percentage in
pretending anything else. That was his mistake last night, or one of
them. He reminded himself that, no matter what, you have to show
strength. If the other person isn't playing your game, then you're
playing his. And that means you're losing. He told her Binion's, the
centre of the universe. She didn't blink an eye. Like she was expect-
ing it.

For some very silly reason he expected her to show up wearing
her wings and halo. So he was slightly disappointed when she
appeared wearing jeans and a T-shirt. Mook was waiting in a booth,
facing the door, and she saw him right away. She walked over and sat
down facing him. 'Hello, Edward.'

'Mookey, I told you my name is Mookey.'

She shook her head, her face stern. 'No, I can't do that. I can't call
you any of those names. Not Mookey, not Ace, or Speed, or whatever. Not Fast Eddie. I'm sick of those names. Can you live with
that?'

He let it go. Another thing he'd learned in the past six months
was that you have to pick your fights. Decide early what's important
and what's not. What's worth fighting for.

They both ordered omelettes with coffee. When the waitress
came by with their orders she paused for a second and then said, 'Oh,
Annie, I didn't recognize you.'

Annie nodded. 'It's been a while, I guess. How are you, Cathy?'

Mook waited till the waitress, Cathy, left and then said, 'Small
town.'

'At heart, yeah it is. Listen, Edward....'

Here it comes, he thought. And jumped in first. 'Why did you come back here?'

She took a sip of coffee and looked around the room, like maybe the answer was there on one of the walls, or on the face of one of the players taking a break from a poker game or the craps table. The coffee shop was a separate room from the casino but open to it, so on top of everything washed the roar of the crowd, the ringing of the slot bells. She cocked her head and seemed to listen to that for a second before she answered him.

'That's a good question. I left because all this –' she swept her arm indicating the casino, the players in the coffee shop, the waitresses with their bleached hair and microscopic skirts '– all this started to feel normal to me. Like this was a sensible way for people to act. So I left.' She was still staring off, not really looking at anything in particular it seemed, but not looking at Mook either. 'But it turned out I still felt that way. Out there, the real world, felt strange to me. I can't explain it. I'm back, and maybe if I get enough of this place with my eyes open, I'll see it for what it is. Be able to move on. I think the only way for me to truly be rid of this place is to fill up on it.'

He was struck by a thought, a memory he couldn't quite place. 'You're drinking yourself sober.'

'What?'

'Nothing. It's just something I heard once.'

She said the words over silently to herself, like she was seriously considering what to think. 'I guess I am,' she said. 'But part of getting sober is not going back to certain places I've been. I mean, I'm back here but I'm careful not to be part of it. Do you know what I mean? That's why I ran out on you last night.'

Mook still wasn't too sure what she was saying, but her face was so sad that he thought his heart would break. 'Look, Annie, all I –'

She held up a hand, palm out, *stop*. 'I can't, Edward, trust me.' She sat for a few seconds, silent, like she was thinking something over. 'You're a poker player, right?' He nodded his head but said nothing, waiting to see what she'd say. She nodded her head too. 'You play what, 10-20, maybe 20-40?'

He considered telling her, yeah, he played in those games, did pretty good too. But he knew that, somehow, she'd know. She'd read him for a liar and that would be the end. So all he could do, not liking it very much at all, was tell the truth.

'No, I'm not ready for those games yet. I play 6-12, mostly 5-10, the tourist games, the small time.' He expected her to smile or at least make some comment, but she didn't. She just nodded, the sad look still on her face.

'That's hard, Edward,' she said. 'Those low-stakes games....' She stared off, like she was seeing Mook's day, every day, play out in front of her eyes. She said it again, 'That's hard.'

And again he found that he wanted to tell her the truth, convinced that she could read him perfectly. 'Yes, it is,' he said. 'I'm finding it pretty tough lately. Not exactly what I expected. But I hope to move up, I'm hoping to move up.'

'You think you'll make it?'

'I don't know. I really don't know any more. I thought I would, when I first got here. I thought it was only a matter of time. Lately, I don't know. I wonder if I have the heart for it. Can I tell you a story?'

'Of course.'

'I was playing in a small game, my game, a few weeks ago. A good-looking table, lots of loose players, and lots of local retirees, old men who sit on their cards, play it safe, let you run the table.'

'Rocks.'

Again she surprised him. 'Right, rocks. And I'm doing really well for once. Making huge money for such a low limit. I'm up almost eleven hundred dollars at 6-12, unbelievable. Because the rocks, and especially this one old guy, keep getting really good but always second-best hands. Again and again we go to the river, the raising capped out, and this one old man, this old pensioner in his cardigan sweater and corduroy trousers, always falls just short of my hand. It was amazing.' He stopped and watched it happen in his mind, seeing the table and the cards, seeing the face of the pensioner growing grimmer and paler with each hand. Seeing him buy back in again and again, each time for smaller amounts, each time counting and recounting first his money then his stack of chips, watching it evaporate.

'And?'

'And, like I told you, I was killing them. I *did* kill them. Eleven hundred dollars. At 6-12, that's just unbelievable.'

'*And?*'

'And the old guy in the cardigan busts out, broke, and leaves the table. I keep playing, of course. But after a couple of hands I walk and go to the washroom, wash my face, you know, to keep fresh. Walking back I see him sitting at a coffee bar. He's got two or three of his friends clustered around him, more old men, and he's weeping. He's actually weeping, sobbing like you only see kids do, completely destroyed.'

Annie held up her hand. 'Stop,' she said. 'You don't have to tell me. I know where this is going.'

'No, I don't think you do.' He saw the old man in closer focus, his eyes red, tears smeared over his cheeks, wiping the back of one hand across his face. 'I was mad at myself, furious, but not for the reasons you'd think. I was mad because I felt sorry for the guy. I still do. And I knew that if I'm going to make it doing what I'm doing, I can't feel that way. If I'm going to succeed here, if I'm going to play the big games, it goes beyond that. I have to be happy when I see that. I have to be *overjoyed* when I see that, because then I know that whoever is crying, I own him, he's mine. That's what it's going to take. And I don't know if I have it.'

Annie watched him, her face completely neutral. Then she smiled and the smile somehow opened her face, allowing him truly in for the first time. She reached out and touched his hand. 'But you have something, Edward, you do have something.' She held his hand for a moment and then released it. She was still smiling at him, genuinely, he thought, but the mask was back. 'I have to go.'

He watched her walk through the casino and disappear. Then he searched out Cathy the waitress and asked her straight out how she knew Annie.

'Annie?' Cathy asked. 'I just do. I haven't seen her in years, but before that she was here more than I was.' Like that should mean something to him. When it was obvious that it didn't, she said, 'She's Annie *Thompson*, man. She's *famous!*' When that still didn't do it for him, she blew out her breath in exasperation. 'Christ, she's only the best woman poker player this town has seen. She's famous, I told you. She's even got her picture up on the wall.'

She pointed Mook towards a wall covered in plaques and photographs in cheap frames, just beside the poker room. He scanned the wall as he got closer, picking out various poker players he did know, if only from 'Card Player'. Puggy Pearson, Johnny Moss, Doyle Brunson, old pictures of old guys showing their blank faces to the camera. The only women he saw were in crowd shots, wives and girlfriends. Then he found her. A faded eight-by-ten in a plastic frame. Annie probably fifteen years ago, hair in a busy perm, big smile on her face. A tarnished brass plate glued to the glass read: Annie Thompson, future champion. She was surrounded by a crowd of famous poker faces, faces smiling for a change, beaming down on her. Johnny and Doyle, on either side of her, had their arms around her shoulders. Johnny Moss and Doyle Brunson, shit. He'd been telling her hard-luck stories about playing 5-10.

'I know who you are.' She was just back at her post under the marquee, back in her robe but not yet in her ratty wings. She held them in one hand, the basket of shitty gloves and her halo in the other. She didn't look too surprised to see him. He said it again. 'I saw your picture. I know who you are.'

She put the halo and the basket down and began to strap on the wings, backpack style. She turned her back on him so he could cinch her up. 'I thought maybe you would.' She turned again to face him.

'For Christ's sake, Annie. What's this all about? Why do you keep running away from me?'

'Edward, I didn't know what else to do.' She paused, her face pained, as if she were looking for a way to tell him something he couldn't possibly understand. She tried again. 'Edward, you *are* me, the me I used to be. I told you I was trying to be rid of this place. If I start to care for someone like you, I –' Again she paused.

'I grew up here, you know that. I've lived my life here. We're maybe a couple of hours from the Grand Canyon. We're an hour, tops, from Hoover Dam, one of the whatever wonders of the world. People come from all over the world to see them. I've never seen either of them. I've never *wanted* to see them. All I ever wanted to see was the inside of every poker room in town. Isn't that beyond pathetic?'

Her eyes were wet now, just at the point of tears, and Mookey had the almost overpowering urge to reach out and stroke her cheek. But he couldn't. Not while they were talking about her and her past, which meant talking about him and his maybe future. 'At one time it must have been what you wanted.'

She stared off for a second, blinking hard, before answering him. 'Maybe. I was twenty-two years old. I was a *kid*. And I was good, really good. I was like some kind of ... mascot to those guys. Like everyone's smart little sister. But that's not enough, Edward, it's just not enough. And I can tell you right now, it won't be enough for you, either.'

He let that go. 'So why are you back, then?'

The tears were gone now. 'Jesus! I don't know, Edward. Look, do me a favour. If you're going to waste your life in this town, at least do it doing what you want, not something that's almost what you want.'

He didn't answer. Instead, he did another mental flip-flop and watched the unlikely scene of himself talking to this grave angel. Saw himself listening and talking, standing in the shadow of the marquee assaulted by the din of the machines, and wondered, truly wondered because for just a moment he didn't know, how he got to be there.

He snapped back into himself and Annie was talking. And, while she still looked sad beyond words, he realized that she was sad for him, Annie was grieving for him. 'Have you ever thought of this: you don't do anything as much as you play poker. Not if you're the serious player you say you are. Not walk or talk, not sleep, not read a book. You sit and you breathe bad air with a bunch of surly cry-babies doing exactly the same thing, waiting to fleece some innocent of another fifty or hundred bucks.

'It starts to cross over, Edward, it has to. To play poker, it's not enough to not care about the money, to not care about the other players. Look at a poker player and his eyes are flat. Like he's one step back from himself, considering his position. *You're* not even a part of it: it's just him and his situation, nothing else. He doesn't care about anything or anyone, he *can't*. I don't think you can do that, Edward. I couldn't.'

'I'm doing what I want.'

Annie snorted. 'That's crap,' she said. 'You're doing something that's *almost* what you want. That *looks* like what you want if you squint hard enough. And you've convinced yourself that it's good enough.'

'I don't have the money. I'm not ready for the big game.'

'Is that the real reason?'

He told her the truth. 'No, it's not. I'm afraid. That's the truth of it. I'm afraid I won't be good enough.'

'OK, then. So how are you going to find out if you don't try? And how much time are you going to waste playing in the chickenshit games until you give up altogether?' She snorted. 'High stakes poker can be a waste of a life, but the games you're playing? Jesus.'

3.

HE SAT DOWN AS someone was just finishing up a joke, one of about four that seemed to float from table to table and that Mook had heard a hundred and fifteen times each.

'So the guy says, "How do I know this money will go to feed your kids and not directly into some poker game?" and the second guy says, "Oh, I got *gambling* money!"' No one laughed, not even the guy telling the story. Just another little ritual gone through, one of any number on a list. Mook signalled for chips.

The minimum buy-in was a thousand dollars, which Mook knew was the real joke. The game was pot-limit, where each bet could be the size of the pot, equal to the amount of money already in there. If the pot was one hundred dollars, you could call the hundred, making the pot two, then raise the two. Now there was four to the next player, who could possibly make it sixteen hundred. That wouldn't happen every hand, or every hundred hands, but when it happened it would happen hard. One thousand was a joke in these leagues and, just possibly, maybe he would be too. For the first time in a long while Mook was nervous. He put his roll on the table, all of it. 'Buy in for six,' he said. Sixty Franklins, sixty one-hundred-dollar bills: six thousand dollars. He might have asked for bus change, all the notice anyone took.

The floorman brought his racks of chips. Red five-dollar chips, nickels. Green quarters. One stack of twenty blacks, one hundred dollar chips, two thousand dollars worth. All the money he had in the world converted into neat stacks of twenty, red in front, then green, then black. He called for the waitress to bring him a bottle of Mountain Valley, pulled his chair in close to the table, and got ready to wait.

A game like this could come down to one hand, Mook knew that. You sit and don't win a hand for an hour, six hours, and it doesn't matter. You wait to trap someone, take all his money. The object isn't to hurt the other player, it's to destroy him completely. And it could all come down to maybe thirty seconds out of ten or twelve hours' play. And in that thirty seconds Mook could win more than in six months of playing low limit. He could lose it too, he knew that. So he waited, careful, studying the other players.

Who were all different kinds of good. Most of the nine were solid, aggressive players, always coming at you. These guys kept pressing, pressing, and would never let up. Which was OK, Mook knew how to handle them. He had a couple thousand hours of Vegas poker under his belt. Let them press all they wanted, he was ready.

One guy stood out because of his non-stop 'woofing'. A huge older guy, maybe six-four and three hundred pounds, grey hair buzzed close to his scalp, he started in on Mook right away. 'Look at this little fuck,' he announced to the table. 'Shaking like a dog shitting a peach pit. Best go home, boy. Run back where you're safe.' Woofing. Which was supposed to throw you off your game. That was OK, too. This guy had it all wrong, or wrong enough, anyway. He tried to make poker personal. The whole trick was to make it completely impersonal. Hell, make it *inhuman* if you could.

Only one guy worried him. He was in the third position, seat three, and was all but invisible, nothing in his face or manner for Mook to read. He had a mountain of chips in front of him, maybe twenty thousand dollars, and looked like he was bored, like maybe the stakes were too low for him. Which didn't mean he was careless. At a table of players with blank faces and killers' eyes this guy stood out. When you stared at him all you saw was yourself, diminished, squinting back. Like seeing your reflection in the blade of a knife.

So he hunkered down. He played tight, careful, throwing away maybe nine hands out of ten before the flop. On the flop, after seeing the three up cards, he mostly folded. Playing tight. Not too tight, though. He'd wait till he had position, with just the right players in the pot, and make a move. Steal small pots by making a good raise. Slow play trips, three of a kind, then hammer his opponent when he came after Mook, pressing. He did OK. And all the time he was studying the other nine, looking for patterns, always searching for weakness. After four hours he had almost nine thousand dollars in front of him.

He took a break. Went to the washroom to splash his face. Walked a lap around the casino. He was getting into the flow but he was also approaching a dangerous time, he knew that. He had to keep his attention every second of the play. Not one other thought could intrude upon his poker. He was up almost three thousand dollars and with luck and good play would make much, much more, but he had to be careful. He walked through the crowd of slot players, blackjack bettors, tourists, drunks, whoever, and didn't see them. All that mattered in the whole world was the nine other men at his table. Them and their money.

On the next hand after he sat down he put the Woofer on tilt. He'd seen that despite his bluster the Woofer was a cautious player. He'd storm out at you, but if you played back in strength he'd tighten right up, often fold. Mook waited till it was just the two of them. Two or three people had tested the water, but when the Woofer raised up before the flop they folded. After the flop the Woofer came out with a bet the size of the pot, making it six hundred. Mook hadn't made a hand but came out after the Woofer.

'Raise,' he said. He counted two off the top of a stack of blacks and pushed the eighteen hundred to the centre. He didn't look at the Woofer, didn't not look at him, tried to do nothing that would give any kind of tell to his play.

The Woofer thought for almost a minute. 'Mother fucker's got himself a hand,' he announced finally and tossed his hand away. Mook swept in the pot and then, blank face to the Woofer, turned over his two useless cards.

The Woofer exploded. He jerked to his feet and screamed, actually screamed, 'Fuck!' at the top of his lungs. Mook thought he might actually come across the table at him. And during the whole tantrum Mook was really only thinking one thing: I've got him.

Ten hands later Mook wound up alone in another pot with the Woofer. Mook raised it up, this time pushing two thousand in. The Woofer didn't hesitate, and came back with his whole stack, pushing in almost eight thousand dollars. Mook looked at the pile of chips, at the three cards in the centre, at the flushed face of the Woofer. 'Call,' he said, and pushed his stacks forward. He felt nothing as he turned over his cards: pocket Kings, giving him three of a kind. Neither the fourth nor fifth cards, the turn and the river, helped the Woofer's hand. Mook's Kings stood up and the Woofer was gone. Destroyed. Mook had almost twenty thousand dollars in front of him. Maybe he'd make it in these leagues after all. He didn't notice the Woofer leave the table.

He kept playing. Nothing as dramatic as busting the Woofer came along, just solid tight play. He took a break for a clubhouse sandwich at hour six but was back to the table in twenty minutes. A couple of the smaller players left and were replaced by others who played just like them. Seat Three remained, still playing dangerous poker. He was a player who would lose a dozen, two dozen pots in order to make one good one. He'd draw to ridiculous hands, hands Mook wouldn't touch at limit poker, because he could set up a huge payday on the river if he hit. In the games Mook was used to it was all percentage play, using the odds to make your money over the long haul. Here it was all about the one big score. Seat Three looked like he could wait all night, all week if necessary. And Mook knew that if he got into a serious pot with him Mook would have to be very, very careful.

By hour twelve he was beginning to fade. He was drinking coffee now, for the edge. Maybe too much edge, but better that than not enough. He thought about what Annie had said, about not caring. And he got just a glimpse, just a sliver of how he was starting to care for her, how much she might mean to him. Then he told himself to get Annie out of his head and concentrate. Now more than ever he had to hunker down inside himself, give nothing away, even if it was to a woman who wasn't even present.

A few more players had cycled through, but Seat Three was still there, still looked exactly as he had when Mook sat down. And Mook realized that he himself was still there, still playing, because Seat Three was. Right now Seat Three was poker to Mook. He'd play till he beat him, or until Seat Three quit the game, one or the other. Either way, it would be Mookey who was left at the end of the day. He'd been through too much for this, given up too much of his life to the tourists and the smoke and the flat-out boredom. This was his reward. When this day was over it would be Mookey Livingston sitting at the table with a King Hell stack of poker chips, no one else.

They played on. Fourteen, sixteen hours passed. Mook's stack dropped by a few thousand, came back up, remained mostly even as he waited for his chance. For reasons he couldn't understand it had all come down to this one game, here, now. It wouldn't be good enough to leave, sleep, and return to the table. It had to happen here, now, and it was inevitable that it would come down to Mookey, punchy with coffee and lack of sleep, and the enigma in seat three. He told himself that no one else could matter.

He thought of something Annie had said, just before they parted. After she'd been slagging poker and poker players and the whole life, she stopped. 'The point of all this isn't that poker makes you a bad person. Some of the best people I knew in this town were poker players. But to succeed at it, to really excel, poker has to become everything, your whole life. And when you stand back from it, stop for a second and stand back, just what kind of life is it?'

Right now the life looked pretty good. Even better because he knew what Annie was talking about. So, just maybe, he could have it both ways. He'd see. Her image stayed in his mind, an image he knew he had to force back out: Annie. He saw her face, her eyes burning at him, a strand of her hair falling across one cheek. Her eyes with their tears not just for herself but for him, too. Annie. He shook his head, took a sip of water, and got back to the business of poker.

He set out to trap Seat Three. With the King and Queen of hearts in the hole, he smooth called a small raise before the flop. Seat Three stayed in, along with three other players. When the flop came down with a King and a Queen and a small heart, Mook knew that his time was coming. The others checked around to him and he bet the size of the pot. Seat Three would know him well enough that he'd read such a strong bet as a weak or at least vulnerable hand. So, by playing a strong hand strongly, he was actually showing deceptive weakness. God, he loved this game.

The other three players dropped but Seat Three stayed with him. The turn card was another low heart, giving him top two pair and a big flush draw. Mook still had the boss hand. He pushed two thousand into the pot and Seat Three raised it by another two. Now it was Mookey's turn to think. Wheels within wheels, what could Seat Three be playing? Mook put him on a pocket pair or, possibly, trips. If Seat Three was slow-playing trips, Mook was staring down trouble. He was also getting respect, since Seat Three was throwing sophisticated moves at him, ones you could only use on a player with enough brains to recognize them.

The river card was the three of hearts. Runner-runner hearts had made his flush for him. Mook stared at the table, counting the time off in his head, then looked up at Seat Three watching him. Mook had him, had him cold, and the only decision now was how to finish him off.

'Check,' he said. It was a risk, but if Seat Three played at him, Mook owned him. In games like this, you played against your opponent's weakness more than the cards. He'd just shown weakness and he had to hope that it was enough to set off Seat Three.

'Bet.' Seat Three nodded at the dealer, who counted down the pot and announced its size. Just over twelve thousand dollars. Seat Three nodded again, then pushed the same amount forward.

Mook held himself still. This was the one hand out of ten thousand it all came down to. The past six months of living for nothing but poker, of tending bar and living in a cracker-box on the wrong side of town, of breathing smoke and eating bad food, of sitting and waiting, all came down to this one hand, here, now. No matter what happened, this was the poker hand of his life. The poker hand that would change his life, forever. With a shiver he realized that he wasn't sure which way he wanted it to go because he knew that every time you gained one thing you had to give up another. He leaned forward and began to push his stacks to the centre. 'Raise it up,' he said, his voice steady.

He pushed his last stack of blacks in, then plucked the top chip from the pile. He held up the single black chip. 'I'm all in,' he said. Asking without asking if he could keep his last one hundred dollars.

Seat Three shrugged, who cares, and began to push his money to the middle, stack after stack of black and green and red chips, tower after tower. And Mook knew with a sudden shudder that it was over. There was better than thirty-five thousand dollars in the middle of the table, a pot he'd played as well as any he'd ever been in, and he was going to lose it all. He wondered for a second if his last chip would have made the difference. If that one chip was what it would have taken to beat Seat Three. It didn't matter. Mook turned over his cards. He had a king high flush. Seat Three, expressionless, turned over his own. The ace and ten, both hearts. Mook had lost to the ace high flush. Seat Three had trapped him. The pro had waited more than sixteen hours, calm, emotionless, inhuman. It was over. And, impossibly, Mookey was just a little bit glad.

Annie opened the door and leaned against the jamb. Mook was once again struck by her beauty. Not the Las Vegas ideal of blond hair and perfect impossible breasts, but the beauty of a real woman. She was half smiling, the almost-smile making small wrinkles at the edges of her mouth, the corners of her eyes. She didn't look all that surprised to see him. 'I don't recall giving you my address,' she said.

'I handed a hundred dollars to someone at the Promised Land,' he said. 'He couldn't give it to me fast enough.'

She nodded, as if he'd just told her the most reasonable thing in the world. 'And?'

'It's over. I'm through with poker. I think maybe I'm through with all of this.'

Again she nodded. 'You lost it all.' No hint of a question in her voice.

His turn to smile. 'All but the hundred I paid to find you. Sometimes the right play is doing the wrong thing at the right time. You know?'

Annie didn't say anything for a moment. Then, 'I didn't really mean all those things I said before, not really.' She wasn't smiling any more, and she managed to stare just slightly over his left shoulder. 'It's o k to have a dream, even if it's poker. Maybe not for me but.... I didn't mean all those things.'

He shook his head, his turn to smile. 'Yes, you did. You meant it for me, too. We're the same.' He caught her eye and held it. 'I thought maybe you'd like to come away with me. For two or three days, whatever. We could rent a car, be tourists. Visit the dam, maybe the Grand Canyon.'

She laughed, shaking her head. 'I hardly know you.'

'We know each other.' He watched her think it over. For the first time in as long as he could remember, he didn't try to get a read. Didn't try to play her. He just waited to see what she would say.

'This isn't about poker.'

'I know. I know it's not poker.'

She smiled again, maybe at him, maybe at the whole situation. Maybe because she just felt like smiling. He realized that, until this moment, when he thought of Annie he felt an overwhelming sense of sadness. And he could see sadness, like a physical thing, begin to fade from her. 'I guess you'd better come in, Mookey.'

He shook his head. 'Call me Edward. My name is Edward.'

Acknowledgements

Some of these stories have been published in *B&A New Fiction, The New Quarterly, The Fiddlehead, Event, Grain,* and *Queen's Quarterly.*

'Oh, Henry' and 'Everett and Evalynne' appeared in *Coming Attraction 96* published by Oberon. 'Steam' appeared in *The Journey Prize Anthology 8* published by McClelland & Stewart.

LEAH SHAPERA

Murray Logan has published widely in literary journals. His stories have been featured in the *Coming Attractions 96* and *The Journey Prize Anthology 8*. He lives in Vancouver.